D0865367

DARK NIGHTS

Copyright © 2017 Read Books Ltd.
This book is copyright and may not be
reproduced or copied in any way without
the express permission of the publisher in writing

British Library Cataloguing-in-Publication Data
A catalogue record for this book is available from the
British Library

DARK NIGHTS

by

THOMAS BURKE

WHAT THIS BOOK IS ABOUT

Thomas Burke's Limehouse stories, from *Limehouse Nights* onwards, are world-famous. That his stories remain absolutely unique is proved by this latest volume in which, against the fascinating background of Limehouse and the Thames waterfront, are depicted the comedy, tragedy, romance, poverty and sometimes crude realism of a colourful, cosmopolitan population. Of this volume might be said the same that *Truth* wrote of *Abduction*, "All the qualities for which he is famous are here as marked as ever—an intense sense of the genuine, dramatic, swift and vivid drawing of character, biting phrases and poetic paragraphs. The author has probably not written a line which has not been first well considered and then brilliantly executed."

BY THE SAME AUTHOR

VICTORIAN GROTESQUE

ABDUCTION

ETC. ETC.

Thomas Burke

Thomas Burke was born in Clapham, London in 1886. His father died when he was very young, and at the age of ten he was removed to a home for middle-class boys who were "respectably descended but without adequate means to their support." Burke published his first piece of writing – a short story entitled 'The Bellamy Diamonds' – in 1901, when he was just fifteen. However, proper recognition came in 1916, with the publication of *Limehouse Nights,* a collection of melodramatic short stories set amongst the immigrant population of London's Chinatown. *Limehouse Nights* was serialized in three British periodicals, *The English Review, Colour* and *The New Witness,* and received positive attention from reviewers and a number of authors, including H. G. Wells. It also sparked something of a controversy, however, and was initially banned by libraries due to the scandalous interracial relationships it portrayed between Chinese men and white women.

It was these portrayals of London's Chinatown that Burke is best-remembered for. However, there is some degree of confusion over how much of Burke's writing was based in fact; as literary critic Anne Witchard states, most of what we know about Burke's life is based on works that "purport to be autobiographical, yet contain far more invention than truth." Whatever the truth, there is no doubt that, in his day, Burke was regarded as the foremost chronicler of London's Chinatown at the turn-of-the-century. Burke told newspaper journalists that he had "sat at the feet of Chinese philosophers who kept opium dens to learn from the lips that could frame only broken English, the secrets, good and evil, of the mysterious East," and these journalists almost uniformly took him at his word.

Burke continued to use descriptions of urban London life as a focus of his writing throughout his life. Off the back of *Limehouse Nights*, Burke published the thematically similar *Twinkletoes* in 1918, and *More Limehouse Nights* in 1921. However, he was a prolific author who tried his hand at a number of different genres. He semi-regularly published essays on the London environment, including pieces such as 'The Real East End' and 'London in My Times', and during the thirties even tried his hand at horror fiction. Indeed, in 1949, shortly after his death, Burke's short story 'The Hands of Ottermole' was voted the best mystery of all time by critics. Burke also influenced the burgeoning film industry in Hollywood; D W Griffith, for example, used the short story 'The Chink and the Child' from *Limehouse Nights* (1917) as basis for his silent movie, *Broken Blossoms* (1919), and Charlie Chaplin derived 'A Dog's Life' (1918) from the same book.

CONTENTS

ROSES ROUND THE DOOR

IF you knew the old Chinatown in the Limehouse and Poplar of the past, you probably knew that little store of. Ah Woo that used to stand at the corner of Korea Street, its window crammed with the spices and the scarlet packets and gay toys of China. A store where you met olive-faced men in lounge suits and bowler hats, whose eyes under the bowler hats held the silence of eastern temples and the glitter of green seas. And where you sometimes met Rosie Moone, the heart-smiter, who was far more of a flower than the Flower Maidens they find for any production of "Parsifal".

The older men gathered in the store to discuss with Ah Woo such matters as high politics and high commerce, with which they had no concern, and which their opinions could no more affect than the opinion of the trapped fly can affect the spider. The younger men gathered to look at Rosie. She drew both English and Chinese around her, and they would stand for an hour gazing upon her and bearing themselves towards her assertively or reverently, according to their knowledge or ignorance of how beautiful maidens like to be treated.

Among those who were often in the store was Cheng Kang. He seldom stayed to gossip. Mostly he came in to make a few quick purchases, as though he were buying remedies for somebody at the point of death, and shot out again before the company realised he had been there. But there were occasions when he looked at Rosie as though he would like to eat her—if he were not so occupied with other eatables. As this was the only attention he showed her, she did not regard him with much favour. Where she killed other young men with smiles, she tried to wound him with stings of the

7

eyes and scorns of the shoulder. He did not seem to notice them.

He seemed to notice very little, and few people noticed him. His only regular associate was old Suey Lim, who lived in Foochoo Street. This perhaps was why few people gave him their countenance. The Limehouse of that time was always noted for its odours. You could in a few minutes catch the odour of bilge-water, of gas, of glue, of resin, of fried-fish, and all those Eastern odours that can almost be tasted on the lips. Some were not too disagreeable. Others were of a kind that required new words to convey their rankness. But if anybody, at that time, wanted a rough synonym for an unpleasant odour, he invariably brought in the name of Suey Lim.

Suey Lim had such a bad name in the district that, with the exception of young Cheng Kang, nobody associated with him but those who already had worse names. He and those about him seemed to have no real occupation, yet they were always making money. He had a finger in most of the pies of Chinatown, and did not disdain even to have fingers in its dumplings and biscuits. Nothing was too small for him, except his hat, and the only thing that was too large was his overbearing manner.

He treated Cheng Kang as a fool, and Cheng Kang went about with behaviour that almost justified the treatment. He was always sad; he appeared to be very stupid; and he certainly was so pessimistic that he could never see a silver lining without thinking of clouds. His manner was so little alert, and he seemed to be such an easy mark, that nobody found it interesting enough to cheat him or double-cross him. He lived in a cottage in Shanghai Street—one of four owned by Suey Lim— and it was understood that Suey Lim let him live rent-free.

What service he gave to warrant this astounding breach of landlord principles, nobody could discover, unless it was the service of publicity agent. Certainly he was always emphatic in his admiration of Suey Lim. Suey Lim was everything that he himself wasn't—forthright, bold, and successful—a fit subject of praise and reverence. He admired him so much that he was always talking in bars about his fine qualities, his generosity, his ability, his sharp wit, his foresight; and he was always so ready to drink his health that he often went home quite tight with admiration.

Suey Lim, on his side, spoke of Cheng Kang as the last of a long line of fools, and often said that his ancestors were no doubt still wandering about in the Middle Air because they hadn't sense enough to go in out of the rain. When they asked why he allowed the fool to hang around him, he said that silent laughter was good for the lungs, and as life provided so few occasions for it, except of an acid kind, which was bad for the lungs, he was grateful for the existence of Cheng Kang, who provided ten occasions every day.

There was a certain day when the fool provided a very special occasion—one that caused Suey Lim to draw in his breath in gusts of whispering laughter, and to ask as much of the world as he could reach to join him in it.

On that day, Suey Lim was poisoning the air by taking a walk through it, when he came to Shanghai Street, and came upon the spectacle of Cheng Kang decorating the doorway and the window-frame of his cottage with paper roses of many colours. He paused to watch and to sniff. Then, with a glance that commanded the attention of those around him to the young idiot, he spoke. He spoke in a loud voice, and in English—for the benefit of the bystanders. "Well, you wooden-headed son of a dough-headed parrot, and what are you supposed to be doing now?"

Cheng Kang politely explained that he was decorating his door and window with paper roses.

"That," said Suey Lim, "could be seen by anybody— even as big a fool as yourself. But I would like to know your purpose in making yourself and your house ridiculous—my house, I should say."

Cheng Kang explained in an equally loud voice that he had invited the beautiful young Rosie from Korea Street to visit him, and take supper with him, that evening, and——".

"What—*you?* Have you got the conceit to suppose that the most desired girl of this quarter, the very flower of the garden, would spend an evening with *you?*"

"Why not? Anyway, she said she would. And so I am making a visible and agreeable welcome to her."

"If that is so," said Suey Lim, "and she has really accepted your invitation, it would occur to anybody but a fool like yourself that it would be only decent to go to the small expense of providing real roses. It is hardly a compliment to a distinguished visitor to greet her with imitation roses."

"In one sense," said Cheng, from the top of a ladder, "you may be right. But at the moment my use of paper roses is intentional, and as Miss Rosie is a girl of brains she will perceive my point. Real roses fade and die. Imitation roses don't. Passion, like real roses, soon perishes. True love, like paper roses, lasts much longer. The three hundred paper roses which I have bought to dress my house inside and out, are not only gay and pleasing to a girl's eye. They are also symbolical of my lasting affection."

Suey Lim hissed with amusement, and the cockney bystanders giggled. "Amiable fool! All that you say with your similes of real roses and passion, and imitation roses and affection, is prettily put, and almost true. But only a fool would tell it to a girl. If you think any girl would prefer imitation roses and lasting affection, to real roses and a brief passion, you are an even bigger fool than I thought."

"You are talking," said Cheng, "of most girls. You don't know Rosie."

"Nor, it is evident, do you." And with that Suey Lim

went on with his walk, shaking with unheard laughter, and told all whom he met of the latest idiocy of Cheng Kang. The bystanders, watching the process of decoration, gradually thinned until only a little girl with a snub nose was left. After much concentrated watching she delivered her opinion on the matter.

"He's right, you know. It's just silly. Paper roses are only for Christmas. They're not things to give to your sweetheart. They might be all right for kids, but any grown-up girl would feel insulted—*I* can tell you that."

"Nevertheless," said Cheng, "I shall go on with the work. You see, it's an old Eastern custom—putting paper roses round your doors and windows and rooms when you entertain your friends."

The snub nose became more snub. "Is it? I never heard of it."

"No doubt, little one, there are many Eastern customs you haven't heard of. Some, I hope, you never will hear of. At least, not until you're much older."

One could not wonder—at any rate, nobody did wonder—that Cheng should have been smitten by Rosie, since Rosie was a rare item in the London scene. One can go about London all day for a week, and seldom see a living creature. Millions of animated phantoms pass along, but only when one of the Rosies flashes by does one realise the meaning of being alive. Rosie was unmistakably alive. She was alive in eyes, fingers, brow, shoulders and shoes, and in the electric frisk of her frock and her hair. Even when standing still she seemed to be dancing, and in movement she was a stream of golden rain. No wonder, then, that when she answered his humble and reverent invitation, by saying, What Next? and then adding—well, perhaps she might: she'd see how she felt: it might be a bit of fun; no wonder he seemed to be knocked off the perch of life on which he had so precarious a footing. No wonder that he was apparently so bemused and distracted by those casual words that he went and bought three hundred paper roses to garnish his dwelling for her delight.

But Suey Lim was right. Cheng did not know his Rosie, or any other girl. And when the story, spread by Suey Lim, came to her that afternoon, she said "What!" in such a tone that if Cheng had heard it, even his slow mind might have gathered that all was not well. Decorating the front of his house, in *her* honour, with *paper* roses! What next—insulting little wretch! What kind of a girl did he take her for? Those foreigners might treat their own women as off-hand as they pleased, but he'd have to be taught that English girls aren't to be treated that cheap way. Buying a girl *paper* roses— when dozens of fellows were ready to give her real roses any day. Nice sort of supper she'd get if his idea of a welcome was to fill the house with paper roses—cardboard pies, probably, and wooden chickens, like a pantomime supper. Go to supper with that little fool?— like fun she would! . . . And a lot more things she said, and worse.

But Cheng was happy in knowing nothing of this, and he went about his preparations with idiotic care, and made such a mess of his cottage that no self-respecting char-woman would have gone near it. When he had, as he hoped, made a perfect setting for the jewel that was Rosie, he took his koto and filled the room and the street with love-music.

The air he played was not a happy air. Love, for him (as he explained to a local lout who asked where the pole-cats were fighting) touched something higher than happiness. He thought of love as a comedy of stings and delights, stings that were sweet, and delights that were tinct with discontent. So his music went into the blue night, carrying in it the dolorous pace of the river, and the aching breath of the exile for the loss of something that was never possessed. It carried a piercing whisper of sorrow and the futility of sorrow.

It sighed of spring-time, and it rippled about despair, and it set the darkness tingling with notes that troubled the ear like the sobbing of a child.

But it didn't trouble Rosie's ear. Like everybody else, she heard it, and like everybody else made blasphemous remarks about it—only stronger than theirs. She was sitting in a café with the favoured boy of the moment, who had money and could hardly, under Rosie's eyes, get it out of his pocket fast enough. If some playboys of the West End are plungers, this boy was a high diver. Rosie was glad she had heard about those paper roses. She was having a good time.

Cheng, at the door of his cottage, went on playing. He explained, to hostile interviewers, that he was listening and waiting for a particular step. Through something like three hours he heard the clitter of many a girl's heels on the stone paving approaching Shanghai Street, but none of them had the vital ring of Rosie's rapid heels. He could, he said, detect hers at fifty yards. But he never did detect them, and as he sat or stood, waiting and waiting, his disappointment made his music light and lissome. Those in near-by streets who had heard his earlier music had assumed that his heart was breaking. They now assumed that his rich uncle had left him everything.

It was past midnight before he realised that Rosie was faithless. As the towers were tolling their message of the end of another and not too-perfect day, he went to the door to give a final look-out for her. The little girl with the snub nose was passing, and he called a question: Had she seen anything of Miss Rosie? She had. She told him cheerfully where Rosie was and what she was doing. He said he had been waiting some hours for her. She said she knew that, and drew the snub nose up to its full height, made a hideous face (which wasn't difficult) and said "What 'opes!" and "What did I tell you?" He ought to have heard the things that Rosie had said about him—that is, if he liked hearing a bit of truth. He asked—what things? She told him one or two of the more repeatable things about himself and his paper roses, and went on her way whistling.

He received her report with Oriental calm. But then, as though he were frantic with self-disgust, he began to tear down the roses round the window and the door, and to tear down the rest of the three hundred strung about the ground-floor room. Then he seemed to realise that if he merely tore them down they would still be lying around for himself and others to see. An ardent lover, in such circumstances, would naturally want to be rid of them; to blot from his sight that evidence of misery and folly. Stamping them into the gutter would be no good, nor piling them into the ash-can. But there is a certain way of obliterating paper; so, at a quarter past midnight, careless of everything, he set about the job.

At eighteen minutes past midnight the dark hush of Limehouse was riddled in three separate places by a fusillade of yellow bells. Those who were about the streets or in the cafés told each other, with authority, that there must be a Fire. In the café where Rosie was sitting, she and the rest of the company got up and went to the door, and reached it just as a young man went running past with news.

"Chinatown's on fire! Shanghai Street's all lit up. The whole dam' street's lit up!"

And it was. In two seconds the café was empty, and the company raced down East India Dock Road to the brightest fire they had seen for some time. Cheng Kang's attempt at destroying the paper roses that so bitterly mocked his wounded heart, had caught his own cottage, and a light wind had carried the flames from there to the three adjoining cottages. Two of these were empty, and from the third the people were able to get themselves and most of their goods away before the flames reached it.

Engines were streaking down the main road, but they

had little chance of doing any work. The elementary History primers used in our elementary schools make such a splash of the Great Fire of London that the elementary minds of builders and surveyors seem to have assumed that that one fire exhausted London's efforts in that way. So, when they laid out the streets and byways, they did so in the bland assurance that there never could be another, and there was therefore no need to make them wide enough to admit a fire-engine.

No engine could get into Shanghai Street. Engines ramped and jingled at the end of the street, and a hose was run down the whole length of it. There was no room for two hoses. By the time the one hose could get to work, the crowd was enjoying the spectacle of four cottages transformed into pillars and wreaths of flame that changed colour with every puff of wind and every fresh bit of material it consumed. Those dull, decrepit cottages went out in crimson, orange, yellow, purple, and white. The fool of Chinatown had provided many a laugh in his time, but his idiocy had never provided so good an entertainment as this; and when the roofs and walls finally folded up and fell, and what had been a first-class fire resolved itself into a black and wet and reeking morass, the crowd went home in a state of thrill and laughter.

Next morning those who hadn't seen it went to look at the ruins. All the young girls, who knew the story, continued to laugh, but one or two older women—old enough to be as youthfully sentimental as youth never is—pitied him. It was natural, after the way he had been treated, that he should want to get rid of the things that had caused Rosie to turn him down, and it was a shame that on top of her treatment, he should have brought this second calamity on himself. They hoped something would be done for him. Perhaps somebody would get up a subscription. If so, that Rosie ought to head the list, and stump up handsome. They sought him out, and while the young girls made a

grinning half-circle about him, the older women con-
doled with him, and patted him, and told him to bear up.

He took the calamity with his usual gravity, and
when they said that something would probably be
done for him, he said it was very kind of them.

Something *was* done for him. A week later he was
sitting with Suey Lim. Suey Lim, who was in the middle
of one of his bouts of teetotalism, was sententious. He
always was when sober. " Well, well," he was saying,
"the gods do as they will with us, and it is all for the
best. We are bothered by business—chastised with paper
roses—and purified by fire. Here," he said, handing
over ten pounds, "is your share. You managed the affair
very well. The insurance people paid on all four cottages without a word. Very soon we shall have another
job for you—over at Woolwich. But I shall have to
think of something new. We can't use paper roses
twice."

SONATA IN SCARLET

AS Hugo Floom turned out of the gaunt Brick Lane into a cadaverous side-street, he heard, at the moment of entering it, a piano making music of a kind that brought him to a stop. It rippled to him out of the night-air like a personal message. It was so much in accord with the many hues of darkness he had walked through that it seemed an interpretation of his mood of that hour. Moreover, it was new. In Spitalfields, that little nest of exiles from Middle Europe, he often heard strange music. This was not only strange but new. Plaintive and pathetic as it was, it had an accent of authority, as though it came from one who knew all the sorrow of the Slav spirit, and was enough removed from it, and had sufficient mastery of his medium, to give it perfect heart-breaking expression.

He stood for some moments looking about the street, and up at the balconies of the tenements. Then he located its source as a little restaurant some way up the street on the other side. Obscure restaurants were one of his little hobbies, and he had wasted a lot of time and acquired much discomfort in sampling every small and outlandish place he happened to see. So the combination of this new music and an undiscovered restaurant was enough to make him march down the street, push open the curtained door, and enter.

Wandering about London at night had long been a harmless hobby of the elderly Hugo Floom, one-time professor of philosophy and an amateur of music. Not wandering about its broad highways and fashionable squares, but diving into its hole-and-corner byways in quarters that even taxi-drivers didn't know, because nobody ever asked a taxi-driver to go to those places. He was in a very real sense a man-about-town, and he would often maintain that no Londoner, whether a son of London or, like most self-styled Londoners, an alien from the provinces, could rightly call himself a Londoner until he could perceive that the breath and pulse of Putney were not the same as the breath and pulse of Notting Hill; until he knew that the voice and speech of Pimlico were not those of Kilburn, and that the colour of Streatham's darkness was different from that of Walthamstow's.

When other men asked him what was the use of such knowledge, when all one needed to know of London was the right restaurants, the right shops, and the right houses, he would snort and say that the acquiring of knowledge was its own reward. He would remind them that Haroun-al-Raschid enjoyed a richness of experience beyond any to be had in the right houses and restaurants of Persia, and would hint that his own wanderings down dim-lit alleys and through dusky open doorways had taught him many things; some of them of peculiar interest and some of a kind that disturbed one's sleep. It was his wandering of this particular evening that enabled him to announce to them next day his discovery of a new force in music; a discovery that subjected him to their bitter scoffing, since before he could produce his genius to silence their scoffing the force had spent itself and the genius had perished. It was just his luck that he had to live with a memory of an experience that nobody would credit.

He had set out that evening, and had marched from Regent's Park to Euston Road; thence across Blooms-bury to Gray's Inn Road, and across that road into the penetralia of Clerkenwell. From Clerkenwell, whose purple darkness, born of its little sloping Italian streets, he always contrasted with the dun darkness of South-wark, he went along Old Street and through interlocking byways he came to Shoreditch, and so into the sad dark-ness of Spitalfields.

At the moment of his pushing open the restaurant door, the music stopped, and when he entered he saw a piano but nobody near it. The restaurant was a one-room affair. Its air was fusty with foreign cigarette smoke and the ghost-odours of consumed meals. It held half a dozen wooden tables and some twenty chairs, and it had a coffee counter and stools ranged before it. Two white-faced black-bearded men were eating some sort of stew at the tables; and at the counter were two ferret-faced men whose eyes and lips seemed to work on swivels, and a broad, husky young man with a thick wet mouth, hard eyes and brutal hands. This man had flat black hair plastered on each side of his forehead in a villainous bang. He wore rings on two fingers. He was dressed in a flashy pull-over and corduroy trousers. He was talking to the ferret-faced men, and was illustrating his feelings about something by spitting on the floor.

Five very ugly customers, Floom thought; and then he saw a sixth figure who was not. Behind the counter stood a girl, darkly lovely. She had a round olive face, shining black hair, and pools of eyes that held all the grief that the music he had just heard had so electrically expressed. Clearly the only hands in that room that could have made that music were hers.

He gathered the scene in a random eye-shot. A man who was not so much at home in remote dark streets might have wished himself out of such a place; but Floom had learned that peaceable men with white hair and benign expressions may go peaceably anywhere; and that the re-assuring feature about gangsters, however tough they look, is that they are interested in gangs, not in individual wanderers. He went straight to one of the tables and sat down. Eyes gave him a second's flash and then left him. The girl, with a step as mournful as her eyes, came from the counter to attend him. He ordered the stew or goulasch, and she went mournfully away to get it.

The black-bearded men at the other table were talking in guttural murmurs simultaneously. They spluttered into each other's sentences. The ferret-faced men were talking in clipped metallic cockney. The brutal young man was talking cockney with a sibilant levantine accent. Such of the talk as he could overhear conveyed nothing to Floom except that somebody had done something he had better not do again. The brutal man spat on the floor, and spat fury from his eyes, and ferocious words from his lips. The ferret-faced men looked perturbed and sorry for somebody—perhaps themselves. Their eyes swung and rolled to and from the door. Every time the big brute snapped at them they seemed to apologise for living.

When the girl brought his goulasch, Floom found, not to his surprise as an amateur of shabby-looking restaurants, that it was good, and decided that what with the music and the girl and the goulasch, it was a place to remember. Its atmosphere might be black with hate and meanness, but that only gave it a pungency of character. It was the kind of place where anything might happen. He found an astringent pleasure in such places, and though experience had taught him that those are just the places where nothing ever does happen, he still went on sampling and hoping.

And then something did happen. The brutal young man left the counter, and began pacing up and down the room, smoking and glaring.

The girl brought Floom a lemon tea, and as she moved from the table she brushed against the young man. He gave a jerk with his forearm against her waist. "Ghat the way!"

The girl gasped, staggered, and moved slowly back behind the counter. She showed no resentment of the blow; only, as she reached the counter, Floom caught from under dropped eyelids a smouldering glow which brought him the incongruous image of flaming ice.

The four customers took no notice. Floom alone moved in his chair, and turned an indignant look on the man. But just as he was about to say something in the

Johnsonian tones with which he had kept his students in order, the man turned his back and went to the piano. And then something else happened. Under those brute hands the piano came to life, and Floom recognized the touch he had heard from the street. It came to life because those hands were the hands of a master. Floom, being a philosopher, was seldom able to control his emotions, and his face registered all his surprise.

What the young man was playing he did not know. It was wild and sad in temper, and Slavonic in spirit, and he was playing it well. Also, like the other piece he had heard from the street, it had the ease and assurance of a masterpiece.

But though he was familiar with all established music, and made a point of hearing the new, this was unknown to him.

Under the influence of the music, he forgot the disgusting moment with the girl. He got up and went over to the piano. When the piece had reached its wild and plaintive end, he spoke to the husky young giant. "Beautifully played."

The giant shifted his cigarette from one side of his mouth to the other. "Huh."

"Yes. It seems to be new. But you played it as though you were thoroughly familiar with it."

"I am."

"Ah. But it *is* new, isn't it? In the modern idiom. But unusually modern. Because it's full of melody, and the composer clearly isn't afraid of beauty."

"Why should he be? It's only the weaklings who're afraid of beauty. They think if they're ugly and formless, like this age, they're being strong. But nobody with real guts is afraid of beauty."

"No. I'm always maintaining that, but none of the young agrees with me. Though the composer of this thing seems to. And the thing you were playing just before I came in. Are they by the same man? They have the same utterance."

"Yuh."

"Ha. He has a great gift of melody. And pathos. What was the piece you were playing before I came in?"

"Just a Night Piece."

"And this you've just played?"

"*Berceuse for an Orphan Child.*"

"But whose are they? I try to keep abreast of current music, but I can't place this accent. I certainly haven't heard them before."

"Nor nobody else. This is the first performance. They was only finished a week or so back."

"Indeed?" Floom opened his eyes. He had certainly stumbled on a place of character; a place in an unknown back-street that could get hold of advance copies of great works. "But I can't relate it to any of the men of to-day: Not Propokieff, I think. Or Bartok. And, if I may ask, how do you come to get hold if it?"

The young giant ignored the question, and snorted contemptuously. "Grr—them chaps couldn't do stuff like *this.*"

"Probably not. But whose is it, then."

"Moine."

"Moyne?" Floom blinked. "I don't seem to recall the name."

The giant twisted his loose mouth. "'Tain't a naime. When I say it's moine, I mean it's *moine.* They're things o' me own."

"*Yours?*" Floom again let his feelings play over his face. He couldn't do anything else, and his face registered surprise, incredulity, irritation, doubt and again irritation. Why was this ruffian telling him such a lie?

The ruffian nodded his ugly head. "Yuh. Me own. And don't look at me like that."

"But—but—you mean to say——?"

The head nodded again. "Yuh. I know what you think. You think I'm a liar. You think, 'cos I don't look like a composer, or talk prop'ly, that I couldn't possibly do things like these. Well, I can. I done a good deal. Got a bundle of things in me room."

Floom stared at the ruffian, trying to associate the music he had heard with the brutal mouth and hands and speech, and the squalid surroundings. Then he realized that he was a fool to suppose that the artist and the work should always be in consonance.

He remembered that grim and ghastly stories are often written by gentle, fastidious dreamers.

He remembered that it was a gross, ill-mannered boor who wrote the clear and sparkling *Figaro* and the majestic Requiem; and that the nineteenth-century arias that carried the sun and colour of Italy round the world came from the sad-eyed morose Verdi.

Looking at the man as he sat with his hands on the keys, he had a new view of him, and accepted the phenomenon. "But why—if you can do work like this—what are you doing here—in this quarter—among——" His eyes moved to the ferret-faced men.

"That's *moy* business."

"I beg your pardon. . . . But this work ought to be known. It should be *done*. You say you've more—like these two things?"

"Yuh. Every now and then the fit takes me. It's a relief, when you're fed up, to do something different. Something you *can* do. Something like nobody else is doing."

Floom, recalling some of the liquid phrases of the Night Piece, again registered bewilderment. A young man with a gift of making spiritual utterance in heart-tearing tones, calling it doing-something-different-when-you're-fed-up. He decided that the man wasn't aware of what he was doing; that it was blind, uninformed genius. Then he remembered the airy dismissal of the two names he had mentioned, and felt that this young man did know. "Those two things," he said, "are masterly."

The ugly head nodded and confirmed him. "Yuh. I

know." There was no boasting in the tone, no satisfaction, no modesty. It was just a statement.

"How many things have you done so far?"

"Seven or eight."

"And none of them published—or played?"

"Naow! Got other things to do. I began about five years ago. I'd always been drawn to music. I could play when I first come to London—I studied till I was seventeen. Then I found I knew more than they did and dropped it. I only took it up again last year. My best thing's a sonata—just finished. You seem interested. Care to hear it?"

Floom was twittering with the story he would be able to tell at the club. "Nothing I'd like more."

The head nodded in recognition of his enthusiasm. "Right. I got nothing to do just now. Come round to my room. 'Tain't far. I gotter better piano there." He got up and turned to the men at the counter. "I'll be back about nine. If he comes, keep him here—see? Don't let him slip. And you——" he turned to the girl. "Keep yer mouth shut. Come on, mister."

Floom followed him out to the dim little street, and into another street, and then another, and then along a passage and into a courtyard. At one of its blank-faced buildings the man stopped, fumbled for a key, and opened a door upon a dark hall. Remembering the appearance and manner of his host, Floom thought, "What a place for sand-bagging!" Then a torch flashed, and he was waved in. "Upstairs. First floor." Floom obeyed, and on the first landing the man went into a room at the left, struck a match and lit two gas-brackets. "Come in, mister."

He went in, and saw a dishevelled but not uncomfortable bed-sitting-room. Some of the furniture had cost money, as they say, and there was no hint of poverty in the various suits of clothes hanging under a curtain, in the gleaming piano, and the bits of jewellery lying on a chest. The room itself was not clean. It was the room of a man who seemed to like living in squalor. Cigarette-ends dotted the floor, and dirty cups which had held tea and coffee stood on the mantelshelf and on the chest and the table; the remains apparently of a teetotal binge. There was a used teapot even on the chair to which the composer invited him. "Siddown, and I'll run over that thing. I don't meet many people interested in real music."

Floom removed the teapot and sat down. The composer went with his spasmodic and ungainly movements to the piano; opened it; adjusted the stool; lifted his ugly hands to the keys—and ceased to be spasmodic or ungainly. Floom forgot the hands, the speech, the behaviour. He saw only a great back and shoulders bowed like the back of a Titan brooding on the sorrow of the earth.

Then from the piano came melody and rhythm of a kind he had heard nowhere else in modern music. It was the melody and harmony of tradition, but used with a modern accent and an entirely individual approach. Just because it was traditional, it had for Floom an air of being revolutionary; yet it was music that could both satisfy the cultivated ear and be instantly understood by the common feeling man. It was as clear as spring-time and as profound as death. It was the spirits of the dead exiles of Spitalfields turned into music. He listened with a grave face and an excited mind. He was hearing in this frowsty room in a back alley of Spitalfields the first performance of what he was sure was a great work; a work that, if he knew anything about music, would create all sorts of discussions but would in the end be recognized as achieving what the modern men were trying for. And he was in at its birth. It would be his discovery.

He had often hoped that his night-wanderings would some time lead him to some discovery which he could exhibit to his friends as a justification of what they considered his eccentricity, but so far the only discovery he had made was that twentieth-century London, though many times larger than the Bagdad of the eighth century, was just as dull as that city before Scheherazade got to work on it. Everything seemed to be open and revealed. But now he had really lit upon something.

The work took about eighteen minutes in performance. When, in a series of phrases that held the grief of the modern world, it came to an end, he sat silent for some moments. Then he got up, turned to the young ruffian, and made a deep bow. "*Maestro!*"

A jerk of the head acknowledged the salute. "Theanks. I know."

Floom smiled, and sat down. "Yes. And yet you're hiding your light. This work should be performed and known. Why hasn't it been? It can only be that you haven't offered it."

"That's right. Can't be bothered. Nothing in it for me, anyway."

"Perhaps you'd let me show it. I'm in touch with all sorts of people in the music world. I know several pianists who'd be most anxious to do it."

"Naow. What's the good?"

"It would be heard, and you would be known. The world to-day needs your gift of melody—your understanding. It needs the poetic emotion that you can stir."

"It don't. All it wants is Tin Pan Alley—stuff as savage as itself. My stuff don't represent it. Don't know what it *does* represent."

Floom thought to himself, "It certainly doesn't represent *you*." Aloud he said, "But why not let the world hear it?"

"'Cos I don't give a damn for the world. I prefer to live the way I do. Life's easy here. I got a racket of me own that keeps me, and I like the life and the colour of it."

"And you won't let me show that thing anywhere?"

"Oh, well, if you're that much interested . . . and if you know somebody who'd see it for what it is—p'raps some day I'll look out the sheets. Can't bother now, though. If you're round this way again, drop in some time. I'm usually at that little café. Or not far from it. Just ask for Pakko."

After that evening Floom went often to the little café. Sometimes he saw the composer, sometimes not. Sometimes he heard him play one or two of his things; sometimes he only saw him behaving like a beast to the girl or bullying the ferret-faced men. Sometimes he saw the master-musician, sometimes the tiger. At no time could he decide which was the true man. And never could he get from him the sheets of the pieces he had played. Always he was put off with a "Can't bother now" and a promise that p'raps some time next week. . . . Only the unique quality of the music kept him on the quest. No amount of trouble was too much to pay for the public excitement of introducing that work to the world, and no man with a thought for music would have been able to leave the affair where it was. So week after week he maintained his visits. And all his labour was wasted.

There came a night when the café was almost empty. The composer was not there, nor the ferret-faced men. Only the two black-bearded men, who seemed night after night to be pursuing an argument that had begun years ago, and the girl. The girl had never given him more than a glance. She had neither welcomed him nor rebuffed him as a regular customer, nor did she appear to notice his indignation at Pakko's treatment of her. But in spite of her cloak of withdrawal he was attracted to her. Her cloudy hair and stormy eyes, against the setting of her smooth olive face, reminded him of Pakko's music; a sonata with the twin themes of electricity and velvet. He found himself speculating about her past and her future; and then he found her speaking to him. In a soft voice, deeper than an English girl's, she said, "What you t'ink of his music?"

"I think it the music of a master."

"Huh. You t'ink it's great?"

"I do."

"Huh. Me also. But——"

"What?"

She shook her shoulders. "Nutting." And then the silence of the dim streets around the café was shattered by two or three quick cries. Floom could never give a precise account of what happened in that minute and the succeeding two. But certain points did remain with him. He saw the door of the café snap open. He saw the husky Pakko dash in and dash to the other side of the counter, and bend down and fumble at the floor. He saw that Pakko had a cut face, and that his light corduroys had a dark stain. While he was still fumbling at the floor, the door again shot open, and two men stalked in. One was tall and alert; the other broad and squat. The tall one went to the counter; the squat one held the door. "Pakko," the tall one said, "I want you."

Pakko vaulted the counter and darted to the far end of the room. "Stop where you are, you fellers. Keep back. You won't get me. Keep back." The tall man stalked towards him. The little room rang with two deafening cracks. The tall man crumpled and fell. The squat man jumped over the fallen man and charged into Pakko's waist. The revolver cracked again, but the squat man held Pakko's wrist and got him down. From the floor came animal snarls, and gasps and thuds. Then the door again flashed open and two uniformed men came in. With three quick steps they were on the strugglers, and with a quick tussle the handcuffs were on Pakko's wrists.

They got him up. The squat man puffed and pointed to the fallen one. "He got him. Twice." He bent over him. "Got him for good, I'm afraid."

Pakko spat. "I warned him. He ought to a-known I mean what I say." With a spasmodic jerk he got to

his feet and made a dash at the door. The uniformed
men held him. He fought them with his hampered
fists, but they held him fast. The squat man gave them
an order. "Take him along." He opened the door
and they hustled him out.

There was one other point that Floom did remember
quite clearly. A point that seemed to him more dreadful
than the savagery of the shooting and the end of a genius.
He had never at any one of his visits seen the girl smile.
Now, as Pakko was led away, he saw her leaning against
the wall behind her counter, with head up and hands
out as though on a hill-top in a sunny breeze. She was
laughing.

On a curdled morning of January two men were
hanged. The report mentioned only one, but they
hanged Pakko, the terror of Spitalfields, and they hanged
an unknown composer. Floom consoled himself with
one thought. The work remained. The manuscripts
of at least seven things were there, in his room, so if
he couldn't do anything for Pakko himself he could
do something for his memory, something that would
mitigate his crude record and his crude end. He would
get the things "done" by somebody, and would write
the full story of them and of their creator. A story that
would make the music world sit up.

He allowed the necessary respectful time to pass, and
then he went one evening to the little café. He found a
different company. The ferret-faced men were not there
nor the white-faced debaters. There were only three or
four men in the place, and they were younger and
brighter, and though the lighting was the same as before,
it seemed to give more illumination. The place was
almost gay. The girl was still there, and she too seemed
to be illuminated. Her eyes were still silent pools, but
they held no grief. She gave him a quiet, business-like
nod of recognition. He sat at the counter and took a
lemon-tea, and in a moment when she was disengaged,

explained his errand and asked about the manuscripts. She nodded again. "Perhaps you come upstairs?"

He followed her upstairs, and in a little room furnished with exotic appointments and decorations, she sat down on a small bed and directed him to a chair. She spoke slowly, picking English words one by one. "You want that his works be known and played?" He said, "Yes. Such work *must* be known." She said sharply and firmly, "No!"

"But—but—work of that quality. . . . To keep it back would be a crime. A crime against music, against life, against——"

"*He* was a crime against life."

"Perhaps. But he was also a genius. Those works belong to the world. They have nothing to do with the crimes of the *man.*"

"They belong to me."

"How?"

"They make up for what he took from me. And they were not *him.*"

"You mean not his own? That he didn't write them?"

"Oh, he made them. They were his work. But they were not *him.* It would be a lie to make the world think so. People would say he may have killed somebody, but he couldn't be so bad or he couldn't have made those things. But he *was* bad. Bad all through. He was worse than a man who kills somebody. He killed people's souls."

"Ah . . . But many artists have been bad outwardly. Their good angel only came through their work. And it doesn't matter what the world thinks of the artist. It's the work that matters."

"But they will—they always do—mix the work with the man who did it. Yes, I know that many artists do silly things—sometimes wicked things. But one knows with them it is not the real man. One knows that the— the spirit is pure. But not so with him. He was never that music. It only came to him, and you saw that he did nothing with it. He was not worthy of it. He despised his gift. He was thief, bully, persecutor, blackmailer. And he died as he had lived—a devil. He wasn't even a fallen angel."

"He may have been all those things. And yet—that music. The world needs it."

She hesitated. The old sullen smoulder came back to her eyes.

"Come," he went on. "Let me have those manuscripts. He was base. You can be magnanimous."

"But—but. . . . He has no *right* to be remembered by that work. Such a man as he was."

"Well—it could be given out under a pseudonym." Again she hesitated, and Floom, remembering the quality of the music, wondered whether some night a little burglary might be possible. It would be no crime. The world had need of the few lovely things it was granted.

"Those manuscripts are mine."

"Yes. But they are things of beauty. Come—won't you share them with the world?"

"They were his. Now they are mine. He took from me all the good I had. They are my compensation. See?"

She got up and opened the door of an iron stove, and, despite his sympathy with her, Floom could have struck her. In the stove was a pile of black ashes.

PROUD MOTHER

WE were sitting in the back room of Old Quong's little store. It was a summer evening, and hot; and a hot evening in the back room of an Oriental store by the London Docks. . . . Manners forbade my remarking on the odour, but I did remark on the heat and on the noise of the children outside. The whole place, I said, seemed to be swarming with children; ordinary Cockney children and half-caste children; and the latter seemed to make double noise—as much noise as the Cockney children plus all sorts of other noises.

Old Quong admitted that the district was prolific, but invited me to look at its amenities and suggest some alternative amusement within the reach of its people. The trouble was, he added, that while women were no more devoted to noisy and blustering children who could use legs and speech, than the rest of us are, they did seem to have deep veneration for babies.

Like that woman (he said) Mrs.—I don't think I ever knew her name—who used to sit about the Tunnel Gardens at Blackwall, where mothers wheel their babies for sun and air.

When I asked—what about this nameless woman?—he said I could make some more tea, and the chrysanthemum buds were in the yellow jar on the second shelf. During the ten minutes of my employment, he spoke two sentences—one about a friend of his who was opening the fifty-ninth restaurant in Soho; and the other about the Japanese, or it might have been the Zoo. I forget. Only after two promptings, and a third cup of Suey-Sen, could I get him back to the nameless woman.

That woman? (he said). Really, there is little to tell. It is not what you would call a story. Merely a slight incident that came under my own observation. Still, perhaps for hot nights slight incidents are fitting, as stories of terror by night are fitting to frost and fog.

I had seen this woman about here for some time before I really noticed her. She was that kind of woman. To me, all Englishwomen are that kind of woman, but I have the authority of various white men of this district—such expert observers in the matter as Young Fred and Big Bill Hawkins and Snooper Jones—that she was, to them also, that kind of woman. The right stature for women, and the stature to which most of your women approximate, is five feet and three inches. This woman stood some inches above this. She wore shoes which Snooper Jones likened to canoes; and the similes which Young Fred contrived to find for her face did more credit to his imagination than to his good feeling.

It was in the Tunnel Gardens that I mostly saw her. You know that open space near Blackwall Tunnel, and how it contrives, despite the neighbouring Tunnel, to be a garden. It was there that I mostly saw her. At that time it was my habit to take a morning walk in the—ah— Garden. At about the hour before mid-day, and in the late afternoon, the sun falls very agreeably upon it— when there is any. And the air from East India Dock blows freely and makes what I think you call a Nice Change from the air of the Causeway. Well, it was there that I commonly saw this woman, and she was always in one part of the Garden—that part where the sun fell most fully—when it fell at all. For it was in that part that the mothers gathered with their first or their latest babies.

It was, indeed, an open-air Mothers' Meeting. One might see there ten, twelve, or twenty mothers, with various kinds of baby-carriage; from the newest neatly-upholstered and well-sprung limousine kind, to wooden boxes, such as my tea-chests here, mounted on wheels. But every vehicle, elegant or makeshift, contained a

c

baby, and in that particular corner of the garden this woman was the only woman without vehicle or baby. She used to sit there for an hour every morning and every afternoon. Just sit and look about her at the mothers pushing their carriages to and fro, or sitting down and dancing their infants on their knees. Then she would get up and go slowly and wistfully away.

Some of the company speculated as to who she was, and why she came so regularly to that corner. She spoke to nobody and apparently noticed nobody. She merely sat and gazed at the little limousines and the sugar or tea boxes. She seemed to have no employment; or, if she had, it was evening employment. She was there most fine mornings and afternoons, and I judged her to be one of those aimless, unattached, friendless women of whom your country produces so many. I never saw her, as I say, elsewhere. When she passed out of the garden she seemed to vanish, so that I sometimes conceived her as a melancholy spectre bound to that one tract of earth. Certainly she was there whenever I chanced to take my walk through the garden, and certainly I never saw her in any of the streets about here.

And then, after this regular and punctual attendance, stretching from one winter to the following autumn, she ceased to come. For many days, and then weeks, she was not seen, and it was assumed that she had moved from the district, or perhaps was ill, or perhaps dead. She had passed from my mind, and no doubt from the minds of those accustomed to seeing her there, before she returned. But she did return, and in slightly different style. She returned in the spring of that year, and she returned with eyes no longer wistful and manner no longer melancholy. She returned with a double baby-carriage in which, under the hood which screened them from the direct sun, could be seen twin bonnets and twin pink cheeks.

She walked proudly, wheeling her baby-carriage round and round the sunny walk. She never paused to glance

at the other women, but wheeled steadily for half an
hour or so. One or two of the mothers, recognising her,
greeted her with smiles, and were prepared to con-
gratulate and compliment her upon the twins, and
exchange notes. But she ignored them. She was as
aloof as before, but this time not in sadness but in pride.
I remarked to myself on the extraordinary change
wrought in woman by motherhood; just such a change
as is wrought in what we call a man when he fulfils his
worldly office of making money. Just as a man blossoms
into strength and poise by this fatuous achievement, so
this woman by her babies was made confident and
proud where before she had been limp and listless.

Her pride broke out on one occasion in my presence.
She was wheeling her children along the sunny walk,
when one of the women, ignoring her resolute and aloof
bearing, or not noticing it, got up and approached her
with some such phrase as women use to each other in
these matters. Something like "Do let me kiss the little
darlings," or words in that key. She was an untidy
woman, not too clean in person or dress, and her own
baby-carriage was of the sugar-box kind. Her approach
was peremptorily waved away. "No—please," the
mother said. "No. I dislike their being touched by
strangers"; and with an offended stare she wheeled
hastily on. The intruder went back to her sugar-box
with a noise of "Cuh!" and questions to the air. Did
the stuck-up thing think, because a woman was poor,
that her touch would poison her brats? There was poor
women who had just as good babies as them better-off—
ah, babies that grew up sometimes and became somebody. One would think that nobody had ever had
babies before, the fuss some people made. . . . And so
on; while I continued to meditate on the parallel of
women with babies and men with thriving businesses.

But soon after this, the woman vanished again, and
this time there was no return. She vanished fully and
completely, and the way of it was this. It was a pleasant

morning of May, and I had just left the garden, and was standing near Blackwall Tunnel awaiting a bus that would take me home. As I hold that Time is the most precious gift the gods have made us, next to life itself, and that waste of Time is a seven-fold sin, I sought to use those empty minutes by retiring into contemplation of the Thundering Silence of Vimalakirti. I was engaged in this when the woman came from the garden, with her baby-carriage, and distracted my concentration. I had not, as I say, at any time seen her outside the garden, and I was interested to note which way she would go.

She stood on the pavement hesitating, with a light hand on the elegant little carriage. And then two louts, engaged in a mock fight, stumbled into her. Her hand was knocked from the carriage, and she herself was knocked against a shop-front. The carriage was facing toward the kerb-stone. It went wheeling down the pavement and over the kerb. Women at a distance saw it going, and screamed. I, being nearest to it, sprang forward to save it. But I was too late. Before it began its flight, a lorry had turned out of the Tunnel and had just put on speed. The little carriage went straight into the head of the lorry.

There were more screams, and hoarse yells, and two women fainted. The driver applied all his brakes, but though his lorry stopped within three feet, the little carriage was underneath it, and the babies were lying this way and that. White and trembling, the driver jumped down, and dived under the lorry. I turned to look for the mother, but I could not see her. Not for some moments.

Then I saw two things. I saw the mother scrambling into a bus that was fleeting away eastward; and I saw the driver with an irritated frown hauling from under the lorry two large pink wax-dolls.

SWEET AND LOW

HOW often (said Old Quong, as I sat with him in the dim little room at the back of his Limehouse store) how often does what appear to be a disastrous mischance turn out to be the key to new fortune. And how often does some little personal eccentricity rescue us from what might have been a dilemma.

Take the case of a young friend of mine, Mr. Dumspike, who used to come here to purchase my best tea, and sometimes other things. Consider the adventure that befell him in Chelsea on one of those Wednesday afternoons that make most of us wonder what it is that has come unstuck.

The young Dumspike (said Old Quong, shaking a few chrysanthemum buds into his cup of Suey Sen) the young Dumspike was of honourable ancestry. I believe your term is Good Family, but it is not quite the same thing; since I so often find that your Good Families have founded their fortunes and estates by backstairs services to princes or money-lending to monarchs, and maintained them by accepting directorships of all sorts of companies. No; this young man was of really good family, with an integrity as unshakable as that of the artist—the highest type of any civilisation, though good families do not always recognise this.

He told me the story of the adventure himself, so I have every reason for believing it to be true, and I can even imagine that some of it really happened.

He was walking aimlessly along Chelsea Embankment on that Wednesday afternoon, looking at the river and the trees, and thinking about the sad plight of his affairs. This was indeed something to think about. I have just told you that he was a young man of good family. It follows therefore that his ability to wrest money from a world that never wants to part with it, was somewhat fine-drawn. His talents, indeed, were of that kind for which there is little or no demand—not even in the West End, where talents unappreciated elsewhere often find a secret market. For his sustenance he was dependent upon the bounty of his Aunt Geraldine, and he was finding this as precarious as the author's dependence upon literature.

For his Aunt Geraldine was a lady with a hard view of life. She expressed this view in her constantly-repeated order to the world at large to Let Her Have No-Nonsense. She held that the young-man-about-town was thirty years out of date, and she expected all young men to work; at least to work hard enough to be self-supporting; and as her nephew, after some years, showed no signs of being capable of this, she was gradually withdrawing her countenance. On his first arrival in town she had allowed him eighty pounds a month, on which he managed to eke out a reasonably comfortable life in rooms in Half-Moon Street. When, at the end of a year he had not secured any remunerative post, she reduced the allowance to fifty pounds. Later she reduced it to forty. Then, finding him still idle, or, as she said, incurably lazy, she reduced it to thirty; until, at the time of that Wednesday, he was struggling along in rooms at Chelsea on a miserable five pounds a week. Further, he had been notified that all that estate which he might have expected to enjoy after Aunt Geraldine had ceased to enjoy it, would go to the other dogs.

But, despite its being Wednesday, it turned out for him a good day, and the little adventure that looked like bringing him to utter ruin was diverted to his favour by one of his personal eccentricities. Namely, a curious habit of writing all his correspondence in pencil on thick large paper. On such small matters does fortune pivot.

Well, he was walking along the Embankment, looking at the river and the trees, when he saw before him the figure of a trim young person in a neat blue costume, with a mop of auburn hair. She walked well, with a poise and bearing that attracted him. Finding the sight of her more agreeable to his eyes than his affairs were to his mind, he turned his mind to her, and followed her for some little time. His active mind was engaged with her swift lines and proud walk, while his sub-conscious mind was ruminating the many things that it might be pleasant to do with that young lady. Then, realising with a start that his sub-conscious was behaving objectionably and Krafft-Ebingly, he shook himself. It was odd, he thought, how these things came into a young man's mind when he was thinking of such things as river and trees and proud maidens tripping along the Embankment. Suppose that charming young person could read his thoughts. How horrified she would be. On the other hand, perhaps . . . But there he was again.

With a movement of the shoulders he shook such matters from him, and at that moment he saw a small white handkerchief flutter from the young lady's bag. Hastening on, he picked it up and pursued her. Drawing level with her, he raised his hat, and said "Pray pardon me, but you dropped this handkerchief, I think," at the same time holding out the handkerchief.

The young lady stopped and looked at him. She had deep blue eyes as large, young Dumspike said, as these small tea-cups of mine, and a bright mouth and a smooth white skin. She looked at him. Then she tossed her head, and spoke. "Blimey, you ain't 'alf got a nerve! Pulling the old handkerchief stunt on a gurl. Can't yeh think of a better one? And what yer take me for, any-way?"

Shocked as he was at the unexpectedness of such language coming from such beauty, he nevertheless, having truth on his side and desiring still to look at her, persisted. "But believe me, this must be your handkerchief. I did indeed see it fall from your bag."

"Grrr," said the young lady. "Lessave a look." She opened her bag, which was already half-open, and looked inside. "Cor! You're right. It *is* mine. There now! Thanks awf'ly. Reely and truly, I'm sorry I flared up like that. No offence meant, see? But reely a gurl has to be so careful—there's so many shysters about, a gurl don't reely know where she's safe and where she ain't. I thought you was trying to get orf—I did reely—but I can see now you're not that sort. They're never as good-looking as you—them sort. And they ain't got your sort o'—sort o' way."

The young Dumspike, on his approach to the young lady, finding that her eyes and face confirmed the impression he had gathered from her walk, decided that she was sweet. When she had uttered her first sentence, he decided that she was low. But on receiving these compliments from her, and on continuing to look at her, her sweetness attracted him more than her lowness repelled him. So he walked on with her, and they talked of this and of that, and he quickly recovered from the shock of hearing such odd phrases and such harsh words coming from so fair a mouth in so clear a voice.

After a while she asked him "D'you live round these parts?"

He said "Yes. Just over there," and indicated a house in Cheyne Walk.

"D'you want a model?"

"Why, no, I don't."

"I'm out of a job just now, see, and I just got to earn something. I think I'd make a very good model."

He looked at her, and his voice confirmed the message of his eyes in saying "I'm sure you would."

"Well, then. . . ."

"But I've no need of a model. I'm not an artist."

The young lady turned on him. "Now don't come it. Telling whoppers like that just 'cos you think a gurl don't know nothing. You just said you live round here."

"I do. But I'm not an artist."

"Coo! You ain't 'alf a one for pulling legs. But you can't pull mine. I know all about it. All the men that

live in Chelsea are artists. I've read about 'em in
novels."

"But honestly and truly I'm not."

She shook her tawny mop and gave him a lovely smile
that somehow made even her strange phrases less ugly
than they would have been in others. "Oh, all-right,
Mister Close-Trap. If it's a secret, I'm not one to poke
me nose. But you can't tell *me*."

"I can only repeat the truth—that I am not an artist.
There are many men living in Chelsea who are not
artists. Ask any of the art critics."

"I dunno any of your fine friends, so how can I? But
have it your own way. It don't matter to me. What
does matter is that I've come over that faint I'd give
anything for a real good cuppatea."

The young Dumspike (said Old Quong) gazed at her,
by his own account, as he would have gazed at an angel
of the Adoration who had come over faint. If low, she
was certainly sweet; so he did what he had never done
before. He packed his lifelong timidity away, and
invited a strange young lady, casually encountered in
the street, to step across and take tea at his rooms. "I
can promise you the tea will be good. I'm particular
about tea."

"Well, I cert'ny could do with a cup. So I don't
mind if I do. 'Tain't orfen you come across reely good ·
tea nowadays—not unless you pay a lot. And I haven't
had anything since breakfast, so a cuppa tea'll go down
good."

Well, they went across to his rooms, and he ordered
tea, and she sat on his chesterfield in attitudes that were
as suave as her phrases were harsh. He sat opposite her
and, so he told me, wondered why the gift of beauty
was so seldom accompanied by the gift of silence. But
he was content to take the low with the sweet, and he
listened without distaste to her remarks on the furniture
of his room, and found compensation in gazing at her.
She took two cups of tea, six sandwiches, and five little

cakes. He was inviting her to take a third cup when she made a remark that compelled his attention from her face to what she was saying.

She looked round the room, and frowned, and nodded as though threatening him. "I cert'ny must say you're a One at playing people up. Telling me you ain't an artist, -when you live in Chelsea, and got all these fine vases in your room. You *must* want a model."

"But I assure you I don't. I give you my word I'm not an artist."

"Your word—oo-er! Lots o' boys give their word to gurls about all sorts o' things. No, I know what it is. You don't believe I'd *do*. But you look here. . . . Wait just half a tick."

Before he could move, she had risen from the chester-field, and in almost one movement had swum gracefully into his bedroom. And before he could say more than "No, but I say——" she had re-appeared.

Yes; she had re-appeared; and there she stood in his room, beautifully posed and, as he expressed it to me, as naked as a Church Bazaar that hasn't got a signed copy of a Hugh Walpole novel. He told me he was struck with astonishment, which I can believe; and with disgust, which I cannot believe. But before there was time for her to strike him with anything else, he was struck from another source. Before he could get out one word of the protest he was about to make, the door opened, and in walked Aunt Geraldine.

Mr. Dumspike did not describe to me all the points of the situation. He said they were too many, and their mental repercussions too various. I gather that he stood still; that Aunt Geraldine stood still; and that the young lady stood still. And then Aunt Geraldine spoke, and said "So!" and again "So!" And then "So *this* is the explanation of your inability to make a career. *This* is why you are unable to rouse yourself to the business of earning a living. This is what you do with the money I allow you. Shameless orgies with hussies. Hareems in Chelsea. God knows what it was in Half-Moon Street. Odious, abominable boy! Never again do you touch a penny of . . ."

"But I assure you, Aunt Geraldine, I——"

"I need no assurance. Nor I imagine do you, or that naked wretch there, who has enough of her own. Explain her if you can."

And then that resource in disaster that had enabled ancestors of his house to turn a lost battle into a victory, came to his aid. He stepped forward and opened his hands. "Really, Aunt Geraldine, it's simple enough."

"She doesn't look that to me."

"But I thought you had heard. I am at work. I am earning a living. I am an artist. This—uh—this is my model."

"An artist? Mmm. . . . Well, my boy, I was always sure you had talent, and I rejoice to hear that you are putting it to some account. But . . . an artist? I see no canvases—easels—brushes."

"Why, no, Auntie dear. I am not that kind of artist. I am engaged in another and more prosperous branch. I work only with pen or pencil. I am an advertisement artist, and they tell me that I shall soon—in their curious phrase—soon be In The Money."

"Well, well," said his Aunt, with a few direct glances at the young person, "that is good hearing. Though you are not, I imagine, from what I see, using this model for drawings for the *drapery* establishments?"

"Oh, no, Aunt Geraldine. No. No. For posters advertising our more select and healthful seaside resorts."

"So? . . . Indeed? . . . Well, well, I have heard something of what has been going on at some of the English seaside resorts of late years. See England First. Brighter Than The Continent. How different things were in the days of our good Edward the Seventh. And so you are making a figure drawing of this—this person."

"Yes, Auntie dear." And in that moment he gave thanks for his eccentricity of writing his correspondence

on large thick paper, and for his habit, when drafting
letters that required thought—such as letters to Aunt
Geraldine—of making little sketches. *Doodles* is, I think,
the quaint modern term. "Yes, Auntie dear." He waved
his hand towards his writing table. "My drawing-
block." And there was a wad of thick large paper, the
topmost sheet being covered with Doodles, mostly of
the female form. "I was just making a few miniature
sketches before beginning work on the full size."

From the young person still posed in nakedness came
a softly-breathed noise of "Coo!" which became a
cough. Aunt Geraldine glanced at her. "Your model
sounds as though she's suffering from croup. This constant exposure, I suppose. I hope it's not infectious."

"Oh, no. No. All these people have something of the
sort. But artists never catch it. We keep a good distance
from them. For perspective, you know."

"Ah, yes. Perspective. How necessary it is—in art
as in life. Well, my boy, as I see you are busy, I'll not
stay. I am gratified that you have at last found something you can do, and have settled down to real work.
My last letter you may ignore. And if you should need
a little more to tide you over until you are what-is-it?—
In the Money—why, just let me know. Now that you
are really getting down to something, you may look
for every encouragement from your aunt."

And that (said Old Quong, filling his water-pipe), that
is the story. Except perhaps for a postscript. Which
is that my young friend, having, for his aunt's benefit,
invented an art career, had to do something about it.
And did. Inspired by his own invention, he showed his
Doodles to an artist-friend in the Six Bells, and to-day
he can command two hundred guineas for posters con-
veying something of the benefits to be had at English
seaside resorts. The figure in the poster is always that
of Sweet and Low, because he has never seen any other.
He married an earnest and influential young woman of
solid middle-class stock, and he introduced Sweet and

Low to a gentleman in the oil business. When he sees her, as he often does, across the room at the Meurice, the Ritz, the Savoy Grill, and places of a kindred nature, they exchange a friendly nod.

Which only shows (said Old Quong) something or other. And now that I have gratified your request for a story, perhaps you will gratify me by going home.

THE PURPLE STAR

THE row began at eight o'clock, and the parties to
it were kind enough to spin it out for fifteen
minutes before it became a fight, and so to give
a chance to a white-haired old gentleman to butt in and
add to the notes of his London wanderings the affair of
the Child and the Purple Star. At eight o'clock he was
four streets away, approaching very slowly the scene of
the row without any idea that a row was on.

Hugo Floom was an ex-professor of Philosophy, but
his method of studying London by night, and the life of
its millions, was scarcely the exact method a philosopher
would have approved. It was indeed deplorably haphazard. It consisted in wandering over the face of
London at dark, taking the next turning, sampling
deathly restaurants and pubs, prowling about alleys on
the edges and in the craters of the Continent of London,
looking in through unshaded windows and open doors,
listening to any talk he might overhear, and occasionally
butting in. His idea was that this noctambulism would
afford him not only good material for a work on the social
labyrinths of the metropolis, but also some contact with
the hidden life which he conjectured behind the multitude
of masks that moved about the streets. Individual
Observation, he held, was far more illuminating than
the most High Mass Observation.

But so far all it had yielded was a few encounters with
people a little different from his own set, and an abortive
discovery of a ruffianly musician. So that the family
row in a remote quarter was a godsend. On that evening
he had wandered across London from Regent's Park
to Waterloo, and then, by way of Bankside, to the
Borough, and into the recesses of Bermondsey. He had
not noticed, after London Bridge, where he was going,
but he knew his London by the different hues of its

darkness and by its various odours. As he set his face
to the breeze, the odour of hops and leather gave him
his location, and he thought he might make his way
home by the Tower Bridge, Bishopsgate, the City Road
and Pentonville. And he would have done that but for
a sudden clamour about his ears that kept him another
hour in Bermondsey.

The sudden clamour was the row, which was deferring
its climax till he should reach it. It came from a short
street on his right, which held about a dozen decrepit
cottages. All the cottages except one were dark and
silent. A clamour of any kind at night was to him a
magnet, and he marched forthwith into the little street
and found the clamour coming from a cottage, right at
the end, whose open door gushed hot voices to the air.
It was not, he decided, the clamour of jollification, but
the clamour of quarrel, and when he remembered that
Bermondsey has an Irish colony, his sense of the desired
poetic harmony between an event and its setting—which
was always being outraged—was this time gratified.

As he reached the doorway, two men went into the
cottage ahead of him. He followed them. He found himself in a small room which seemed to be as uncomfort-
ably crowded as one of Lady Mph's intimate little
receptions. Actually, a quick counting, including himself, brought him a thought of We are Seven. There were
two youngish men, a big, dark-haired woman, a small,
fair girl, and the two older men whom he had followed.
A chair was lying on the floor, a red cloth was half off
the table, and a flower-vase was lying in fragments. One
of the youngish men, with ginger hair, was asking a
question in a grieved voice. "Yes, but who put the gas
out? That's what I want to know. Who put the gas
out?"

The man next him, thin and lanky, said, "How should
I know?"

Ginger snapped. "It was here—on the table. Just
here it was. And it ain't here now. You can do a lot

o' things in the dark. You and Maggie was always like cats for seeing in the dark. Who put the gas out, eh?"

One of the older men spoke in a squeaky voice. "Cats can't see in the dark. That's been proved by scientific——"

The lanky man said, "Shut up, you. Who wants your opinion?" And to Ginger: "Take yer hand off my arm. Take yer hand off, will yeh!"

"Sure. When I got me own. It was on the table. Just here. And who put the gas out, I'd like to know? Come on, now—either you or Maggie——"

The big woman put her hands on her hips in an attitude of challenge.

"Meaning me? Another word from you, Mike, about this, and I'll sock you one."

"Can't help it. It was here before the gas went out. And it ain't here now. That's all I know."

The other older man whom Floom had followed put a plaintive question. "Could it be that ye've lost something?"

Ginger jerked a tight-lipped face towards him. "It could be. And it could be that it'd be a beautiful thing to lose your miserable mug."

Beyond a brief glance, none of them paid any attention to Floom. The men at the door seemed to take him as belonging to the family. The family seemed to take him as the third of a trio of old men. Only the child, who was in the shadow, cold-faced and poised in the frozen repose of a statuette, gave him a settled look, as though aware of an intruder and trying to weigh him up. Ginger went on with the row. He shook the thin man. "Now, Pat, I want an explanation."

The old man who knew about cats said, "Explanations never really settle anything."

Ginger snapped again. "Will yeh mind yer own business? Now then, Pat, where's my star? I want my star."

The old man put his hand in his pocket. "I got the *Evening News* here, mister, if——"

"Shut up. Now, Pat, where's my star?"

"How should I know?"

"It was here a minute ago. Before the gas went out. And it ain't here now. And it ain't the first thing I've lost in this room."

"The only thing you've ever lost here is yer temper."

"I've lost me star. There was only ourselves here and——"

The lanky man thrust his face at Ginger's. He wagged his head with menace, and spoke slowly. "Are you suggesting that your sister and me is capable of——"

"Capable? I wouldn't put nothing past you two."

And then the fight was on. Ginger took two blows—a left from the man, and a blow from the woman that started as a right swing and finished as something between an upper-cut and a strangle-hold. He pushed his sister behind him, where she made the strangle-hold complete, and landed a half-arm jab on the man. The man retorted with two quick straight lefts to the nose, and then Floom's close attention to the display was distracted by a movement on the part of the child. While the three were struggling, he saw her, in the shadow by the window, very gently and slowly lower herself to the carpet, near the bits of broken vase, snatch up something, and thrust it into the top of her stocking. He caught one glimpse of the thing—enough to see that it was not a piece of the broken vase. He caught a flash of gold and purple which recalled to him something he had read a few days earlier in the news.

Then the old man next him, seeing the woman's arm round Ginger's neck, said, "This ain't fair play. Come on!" and made a dive at the woman's waist. The other old man said, "Separate 'em! Separate 'em!" and dashed in and brought them all closer together and himself to the floor. The woman stumbled over him and carried Ginger down with her. As the fight moved towards the corner where the child stood, Floom saw a chance to interfere and perhaps learn something. He

D

had lost interest in the quarrel of the adults. His interest now was in the cold-faced child. The cause and clue of the quarrel might, he thought, be with her.

So he wriggled his way through the scrum, and took her by the arm. "Come on, young lady. Better get out of this or you'll be trampled to nothing. Come on. There's a snack-bar down the street. We'll have a lemonade while they settle it."

At first the child made to jerk away from him. Then, as she found his grip too firm, she let him lead her out of the scrum and out to the street. As they went along, he kept his hand on her shoulder. She looked once at him, and then at the hand, and raised her eyebrows, but made no attempt to break away. "I saw a bright little snack-bar," he said, "just on the left here."

She made a "face". "That one's no good. Nobody goes there. The real one is the Devil's Delight—on the right."

"Very well. We'll go to the Devil's Delight."

"Good. They got ices there. The other one hasn't."

The Devil's Delight was much chillier than its name implied, and scarcely any of the local devils were lending warmth to its marble-topped tables. The child led the way in, seated herself with an air of insouciance, and said she would like a strawberry ice. Floom ordered it, and for himself a coffee, and she told him to cancel it, and order lemonade, 'cos the lemonade would make him less sorry for himself than the sort of coffee they served there. So he ordered lemonade, and asked her whether her family often quarrelled. She said not often; only about twice a week, unless there was some special reason.

Despite her expressionless face, he found her alive and intelligent; too much alive, he thought later. She had the freshness and simplicity of childhood, and with them a manner seriously adult and self-possessed. They talked about Bermondsey, and she told him about her school, and about her taste in films; and that her name was Eileen; and all the time her eyes never left him.

He had the feeling of being looked at by a doctor or a detective.

But when the ice was finished, he remembered that it was he who was to be the detective; so at that point he leaned forward and spoke very quietly. "And now, young lady, suppose you hand over to me the Countess of Lardpan's amethyst star. You have it in your stocking."

The young lady's face registered no surprise or dismay. She just gave him a very long look from her shrewd but clear eyes. "And suppose, old gentleman, I don't?"

"Why, if you don't, I——" He had to stop there. He realized that he had no answer to the question. He fumbled for one; for anything that would have the ring of authority or threat. "Why, I—in that case—why, I'm afraid I shall have to hand you over to the police."

She remained imperturbable. "For an old man, you've certainly got a nerve. Asking me to hand things over to you—someone I've never seen before—a complete stranger. Is that your racket—the kinchin lay? Taking sixpences away from children who've been sent shopping?"

He gave her his sternest professorial look, but it slid off her. "I am not engaged in what you ca l—ah—a racket."

"And yet you drop out of nowhere, and bring me here for ices and ask me to hand over things. You must be on *some* racket. Working for some smasher, perhaps?"

"I work for nobody. If you wish to know, I am a retired professor."

"Mmmm—yes—you've made up pretty well for it. It's a good idea, but it's been done before."

"I repeat that I am a retired professor. And my only purpose in ordering you to hand over that jewel is that I may restore it to its rightful owner."

"It hasn't got one."

"Don't tell me that. As you picked it up, I saw that it was a gold and purple star. Last week there was a burglary at the Countess of Lardpan's house. Among the missing jewels was a gold star set with purple amethysts. Now then!"

"Well?"

"Are you going to hand over that star, so that I may restore it to the countess?" (He saw himself to-morrow at the club, the centre of a group. "Yes, sir. My night-wanderings are sometimes productive. Alone and un-aided. I was able to recover the countess's amethyst star.")

The child, still imperturbable, said: "She wouldn't thank you if you did."

"You will allow me to judge of that. Either you hand it over now, without fuss, or you come with me to the police."

"You got a lot of time to waste, haven't you?"

"My time is my own. Do you want to go to the police station?"

"O.K. with me. Only, d'you know what the police'd do if you took me round there and showed them what I got in me stocking?"

"Why—ah—no."

"They'd hoof you out on your ear for an interfering old busybody, wasting their time."

Floom's bushy eyebrows shot up. He was not used to this manner from adults, and certainly not from children. He put all his authoritarian force into his tone with "*Indeed!*" and received for answer: "Oh, definitely. They hate having their time wasted."

"H'm. And why should I be wasting their time? I should want something more, my child, than *your* word. Remember, I saw you do a deliberate act of theft."

"Wrong again!"

"*Really!* This impertinence. I saw it with my own. eyes."

"You saw me pick up something all right. But you ought to be careful of your words."

For an elderly lecturer on philosophy to be told by a

girl of thirteen to be careful of his words was to Floom
such a phenomenon that he mentally added it to the
few striking things his night-wanderings had thrown
up.

"If it wasn't theft, what was it? What have children
to do with expensive jewellery?"

"Nothing, far's I know. Can I have another ice? I'd
like a Bermondsey Buster this time."

"Er—yes. Nothing, you say? Then what is the
Countess of Lardpan's jewel doing in your stocking?"

The child lifted her head, shook it, and sighed. "Countess of Who's-it me foot! I got nobody's jewels in me
stocking, Santa Claus."

Floom assumed his sternest classroom manner. "Then
what is it you have in your stocking?"

"I don't know why I'm answering all these questions
from an old gentleman. But you're not a bad old stick,
and the ices are good. So I'll tell you, Santa Claus,
what's in me stocking. Nothing but me leg."

"I saw you put a gold and purple star there."

"Well, there's no gold and purple star there now."

"Then where is it?"   .

"You're not doing the professor business too badly.
But you're new, I reckon. You're overdoing it. You
know quite well it's in your pocket."

"*My pocket!*"

"Ur. You talk about me stealing, but I think it's
much worse for an old gentleman like you to go about
stealing—don't you? I should be ashamed of meself,
if I were you. If the police were to——"

But Floom was not listening. He was fumbling furiously
in his pockets, and then, with a gasp, he brought from
the right-hand pocket a gold star set with amethysts.
"You little *fiend*! There's nothing now but to go straight
to the police."

"I'll come with you. It's a fine evening, and it hasn't
been much fun so far. It'll liven things up a bit to see
you hoofed out."

"What is this you keep saying about hoofing out?"

"Only that I reckon the police know more about jewellery than you seem to. That's a gold star, is it, with what-ye-call-'ems?"

"It is. It's the Countess of Lardpan's star."

"Grrr——"

Floom again fumbled. He was aware that this child was at each point making him lose face, and the knowledge of this made him quite awkward in trying to regain it.

"It's quite clear that is what it is. Nothing that a child could say would make me think otherwise. I should want——"

At that moment he half jumped from his chair. The child, with two fingers at her mouth, had let out an ear-splitting whistle. The fly-blown attendant at the counter looked over at her. "What's biting you, young 'un?"

"Just a minute. Something to show you."

He took the time to light the dead half of a cigarette, and came over. She took the star, which Floom was holding, and passed it to him. "What d'you make of that?"

He turned it over in his hand; took it to the light, and turned it again. He asked a question: "Sixpenny store?"

"No. But what d'you make of it?"

He tossed it to the table and went back to the counter. "Gun-metal, gilt. And bottle-glass, treated with oxide of lead. Not badly done. I've seen worse."

Floom was abashed. He felt that the child had made a fool of him, while suspecting that he had made a fool of himself. Without any of his professorial tone, he asked quietly for information. "Is this man an expert?"

"Should be. He was in the trade for some time—till the trade lost too much by him."

"Dear—dear. The things you know! May I ask one more question?"

"I can't stop you. But why should I answer it? How do I know what you are—whether you're on a racket—or perhaps from the police?"

Floom became earnest, even appealing, and shy. Before he knew what he was doing, his interest in the affair led him to explain himself to this child. His tone was apologetic. "I assure you, young lady, on my honour, I am none of those things. I assure you I shall make no use of anything you tell me in confidence. I would just like to hear what story was behind that quarrel—that's all. I'm just a curious old man who likes rambling about London, and looking on at things. I *am* a professor. Here's my card." He passed her one of his cards, which she examined quizzically. "And here is a photo of myself with some of my students." He handed her a press cutting. "Now—will you tell me the story? I promise you that no harm will come to you or your people through me. You can trust me."

She gave him one of her cold but not unfriendly looks, and said: "I believe you. Shoot!"

"Well, what I'd like to know is what you're doing with this imitation of a famous jewel, and why you picked it up when they were all fighting about it."

"If you must know, I was doing my good deed for the day. I was saving my beloved uncle from making a double-size ass of himself."

"Your beloved uncle?"

"Um. The ginger one with the boss-eye. I love him. I adore the way he looks at you when you're in front of him as though you were round the corner of the next street."

"And how was he going to make a—ah—what silly thing was he going to do?"

"He was going to try to work a switch."

"Work a switch? What's that?"

"You know what I mean!"

"I really don't. You're far beyond me in so many things."

"You don't? What are you professor *of*? He was going to work a switch. He got to hear of the man who's got the real purple star, and——"

Floom started. "What! Knows the man who's got the—but the police ought to know of this."

"Now, now. Don't be so fond of butting in. It'll get you into trouble one of these days. And after your promise."

He subsided. "I'm sorry. On the spur of the moment, I forgot. Pray go on. I assure you I have no real intention of mentioning the matter."

"Wouldn't help if you did. What could you tell the police? You couldn't tell 'em who the man is. Nor could I. I don't know who he is."

"But your uncle does, you say. Couldn't they, if they got hold of him, compel him to tell them. I don't know very much about procedure in these matters. I'm just asking."

"They'd get nothing out of Uncle Mick anyway. If they said they'd heard it from a white-haired old f—old gentleman, who'd had it from a kid, uncle'd say it was just a tale made up by a kid who wanted to be thought wide. And I'd admit it. If you're going to talk about police, though, I shan't tell you any more."

"I'm sorry. They'll hear nothing of this through me. Not a syllable. I'm beginning to admire your resource in dealing with situations. I've never met a child like you."

"I don't suppose you have. They must be all dead ones where you come from."

"But what is this thing called a switch? I thought it was something ladies used in their hair."

"When did they? I've never heard of it. The switch, silly, is done like this. I told you he knows who's got the real purple star. So yesterday he made this one, from the picture in the papers, and thought he could go to the man, and tell him he knew a fence who'd give a better price than the others. And the man would bring it out, and while uncle was looking at it, he'd work the switch."

"But what *is* the switch?"

The child tch'd. "Didn't your mother ever tell you anything? Pick up the real one to look at, palm it, and put down the snide one."

"Snide?"

She lifted her eyes to the ceiling. "Goodness! Talking to you's like talking to a baby. I never really thought you were on a racket. Nobody playing simple'd be quite so simple. Snide, old man, snide—meaning dud, flash, stumer, phoney. Got me now?"

"I—ah—begin to understand. So he was going to—ah—work a switch. And you wanted to stop him?"

"That's the idea."

"Ah. I'm glad to know I was mistaken. That you've not been tainted by your surroundings, as I thought at first. I'm glad somebody in your home respects law and order."

"What on earth you talking about? Law and—— I *had* to stop him for his own sake. You see, he's such a fool. I adore him, but he's a complete fool and don't know it. So I have to look after him. He thinks he can be one of the boys, and I know he can't. He's got no more chance of working a switch than you have of pulling a fast one on me. He couldn't switch a good pound-note for a dud sweep-ticket. I knew he'd only land himself in a mess. So when he had it on the table, I turned out the gas when no one was looking, and grabbed it. I guessed he'd never know, and would think it was daddy. Only I dropped it. But when the scrap began, it was easy to pick it up. Only then you butted in and spotted me. Still, it's meant a couple of ices, and no harm done. He's lost his star, and it'll be a lesson to him not to try to be what he's not fit for. Anything more you'd like to know?"

"I'd like to learn a little more about switching. But it really isn't important. D'you think the fight will be over by now?"

"I should think so. None of 'em's much good at it. They can't last more'n a few rounds. Anyway, I'd better be getting back. My beloved uncle may want patching up."

Floom indicated the star. "And what are you going to do with that?"

"That? Oh, you can have that. Perhaps you can get rid of it somewhere, away from here."

"Very well." He slipped it into his pocket, and they went out. At the corner of the little street he thanked her for an interesting and illuminating talk, and gave her an approving pat. "I hope your beloved uncle will profit by his niece's efficiency and fidelity. From what you tell me of him, he has a better niece than I think he deserves."

"He couldn't have. He's an angel. Good night."

She shot into the little street, and Floom crossed the road and went slowly along Tower Bridge Road towards the bridge, thinking over the sidelights he had been granted on a, to him, new world. At the beginning of the bridge, he paused to take in the view both up and down stream, and to note the fall of the moonlight on the buildings of the Tower. Then he walked on. About the middle of the bridge he paused again to feel in his pocket for his pipe, when his hand touched the star. Better, he thought, to get rid of such a thing, in case one fainted or was run over, and the replica of a missing jewel was found on one. He lit his pipe, put his hand over the parapet, and let the glittering thing fall into the deep middle of the river.

He had just done this, and was moving on, when he heard behind him an ear-splitting whistle such as he had heard before. He looked back, and saw a whirl of frock, legs and yellow hair pelting towards him through the silver dark. "Old boy! Old boy!" She reached him gasping. Her insouciance was gone. She was just an agitated child. "Wh-what was that you—dropped over—the bridge?"

"Why, that star thing."

"Bless you. Thank goodness it—it's out of—the way."

"Why? Is there any trouble about it?"

"Might a-been. If you'd done—anything with it—except drown it. Might—ameant a lot of trouble."

"I thought myself it would be better to get rid of it. But why are you so anxious about it?"

"Well, you see—I've just been—talking to—my beloved uncle. And I didn't think it possible—but—I found he'd already made the switch. That star was the real one."

Floom stepped back to the parapet. "Good heavens! What have I done? Accessory——"

"You've put it where it can't trouble my beloved uncle. You've——"

"*Blast* your beloved uncle!"

THE BLOOMSBURY WONDER

A S that September morning came to birth in trembling silver and took life in the hue of dusty gold, Mendel swore.

He had risen somewhat early, and was standing at the bathroom window of his Bloomsbury flat, and was shaving. He first said something like *Ouch* and then something more intense. The cause of those ejaculations was that he had given himself the peculiarly nasty kind of cut possible with some kinds of safety-razor, and the cause of the cut was a sudden movement of the right elbow, and the cause of that was something he had seen from the window.

Through that gracious gold, which seemed almost like a living presence blessing the field of London, moved a man he knew. But a man he knew transformed into a man he did not know. He was not hurrying, which was his usual gait. He wasn't even walking. He was sailing. There was rapture in the lift of the head, and the step was a schoolgirl step. His whole being expressed the emotion that overwhelms the soul in the moment when time stands still and life and the world are isolated and crystallised in well-being.

He seemed to be the one creature of purpose and understanding in a swarm of futile organisms; and this was so alien to the man, so sharply out of character, that it gave Mendel's right arm a shock. For really, as he had always known that sailing figure, he was so much a thing of cobweb and quiver that he belonged to twilight rather than break of day. To see him walking so, in the morning sun, was like seeing one's old boots turn into dancing shoes.

He was tall anyway, and was so thin, and his clothes fitted so tightly, that he seemed of abnormal height. He wore a black double-breasted overcoat, buttoned at the

neck, black trousers and a nondescript hat. He held his
arms behind him, the right hand clasping the elbow of
the left arm. His slender trunk was upright, and his
head thrown back and lifted. In the dusty sunlight he
made a silhouette. Mendel saw him in the flat only,
and he realised then that he always had seen him in the
flat; never all round him. The figure he cut in that
sunlight made Mendel want to see round him, though
what he would find he did not know and could not guess.
And to this day he doesn't know and can't guess.

In conventional society he would have been labelled a
queer creature, that Stephen Trink; but the inner quarters of London hold so many queer creatures, and Mendel
had so wide an acquaintance among them, that Trink
was just one of his crowd. He could never remember
how he came to know him, but for some five years they
had been seeing each other about twice a week. Mendel
liked him almost at once, and the liking grew. Though
he was always aware, in Trink's company, of a slight
unease, he took every opportunity of meeting him.
Trink charmed him. The charm was not the open, easy
charm of one's intimate friend; they never reached that
full contact. It was more spell than charm; the attrac-
tion of opposites, perhaps. Mendel never could analyse
his unease. Beyond a hint of knowing things that others
couldn't know, there was nothing really queer about
Trink. If he was at all odd, it was no more than the
conventional oddity of Bloomsbury. His only marked
characteristic was a deep melancholy, and when, later,
Mendel tried to recall him he found that that was the
one clear thing he could recall. He was one of those
men whom nobody every really knows, and who do not
mean to be known. In talk, he appeared to open his
heart, but Mendel knew very well that he didn't. There
were always covered corners, and nobody could say
surely that Trink was this kind of man or that kind.

Without being at all mysterious, he was a mystery.
Indeed, it was his very "ordinariness" that made him

so baffling. With the man of sudden twists and complexities, or the man of bizarre habits, people know where they are. The foibles, the secrecies, the explosions are sign-posts to character. But with the ordinary man—a scarce type—there is a desert; and when this ordinary man does extraordinary things, it is a desert of an unmapped country. Trink would have been passed over in almost any company, and usually was. Only when Mendel directed his friends' attention towards him, did they recollect having met him and examine their recollection; and then they were baffled. He had once asked five friends in turn what they thought of him, and was given pictures of five totally different men, none of whom he had himself seen in Trink. Each of them, he noted, had to hesitate on the question, and stroke his hair, and say: "Mmm . . . Trink. Well, he's just an ordinary sort of chap—I mean—he's a sort of——" Then, though he had been present ten minutes ago, they would go on to draw a picture as from some hazy memory. They seemed to be describing a man whom they weren't sure they had seen. Their very detail was the fumbling detail of men who are uncertain what they did see, and try to assure themselves by elaboration that they did at any rate see *something*. It was as though he had stood before the camera for his photograph, and the developed plate had come out blank.

In appearance he was insubstantial, and, with his lean, questing face and frail body, would have passed anywhere as an insipid clerk. He stressed his insipidity by certain physical habits. He had a trick of standing in childish attitudes—hands behind back, one foot crooked round the other—and of apparently going to sleep if you looked suddenly at him; and, when speaking to you, of looking at you as though you were his confessor. He had, too, a smile that, though it sounds odd when used of a man, was often described as winsome. The mouth was sharp-cut, rather than firm, and drooped at the corners. His hair was honey-coloured and in short curls. His voice was thin, touched with the east wind; and it was strange to hear him saying the warm, generous things he did say about people in the sleety tone that goes with spite. To everything he said, that tone seemed to add the words—Isn't it disgusting? If he said of any work of Mendel's that it was quite a good thing, the tone implied that it was disgusting of Mendel to do good things. If he said that it was a glorious morning, one felt that it was disgusting of mornings to be glorious. His eyes, behind spectacles, were mild and pale blue. Only when the spectacles were removed did one perceive character; then one could see that the eyes held curious experience and pain.

Wherever he might be, he never seemed to be wholly *there*. He had an air of seeming to be listening to some noise outside the room. He would sit about in attitudes that, since Rodin's Penseur, we have come to accept as attitudes of thought; but if at those times Mendel looked at his face he saw it was empty. He was not thinking. He was brooding. Though indoors he was languid and lounge-y, and his movements were the movements of the sleep-walker, in the street his walk was agitated and precipitous. He seemed to be flying from pursuit. One other notable point about him was that, quiet, insignificant, withdrawn as he was, he could be a most disturbing presence. Even when relaxed in an arm-chair he somehow sent spears and waves of discomfort through the air, sucking and drying the spirit of a room and giving those about him an edge of unease.

What his trouble was—if his melancholy arose from a trouble—he never told Mendel. Often, when Mendel urged him, flippantly, to Cheer Up, he spoke of This Awful Burden, which Mendel dismissed as the usual expression of that intellectual weariness of living which is called "modern", though, like most modern attitudes, it dates from centuries back. He had private means by which he could have lived in something more than comfort, but he seemed contented with three rooms in

the forlorn quarter where Bloomsbury meets Marylebone
—well-furnished rooms that one entered with surprise
from the dinge of Fitzroy Square. He was a member of
two of the more serious clubs, but used them scarcely
twice a year. His time he employed in the Bloomsbury
and Marylebone fashion—as an aimless intellectual. It
is a common type; the elder Oxford or Cambridge that
has never grown out of its second year. In the course of a
lifetime they write one novel or one volume of poems or
essays, and for the rest they write appreciations of obscure
writers in obscure papers that don't pay their writers.
They are to be recognised by their somewhat pathetic
air of superiority and distinction. They have the outward appearance that the popular imagination gives to
the creative artists, only no creative artist is ever half so
distinguished in appearance as most of these translators
and reviewers and art critics. Trink had not written a
novel, but he did write metallic studies for all sorts of
metallic Reviews; and all the time he was doing it he
affected to despise himself for doing it and to despise
the breed with whom he mixed. He attended all their
clique and coterie gatherings—teas, dinners, Bloomsbury parties, private views—and took part in all the
frugal follies of the Chelsea Bohemia. He was seen, as
they say, everywhere. Yet at all those affairs, though
he looked younger than most of the crowd, he had always
the attitude of the amused grown-up overlooking the
antics of the nursery.

Though not physically strong he had immense vitality,
which he exhibited in long night walks through London.
This was a habit which Mendel shared with him and
which, begun in childhood, gave him his peculiar and
comprehensive knowledge of the body and soul of London.
It was on one of those night-wanderings that they had
first met, and later, knowing that Mendel was an early
riser, he would sometimes, at the end of one of those
rambles, call in for breakfast, and then go to sleep on
his chesterfield.

Another of their points in common was a wide range of friendships. Most men find their friends and acquaintance among their own "sort" or their own "set", and never adventure beyond people of like education, like tastes and like social circumstances. Mendel had never been able to restrict himself in that way, nor had Trink. They made their friends wherever they found them, and they found them in queer places. An assembly of all their friends at one meeting would have surprised, and perhaps dismayed, those of them who knew the two men only as writers in such-and-such circumstances. Mendel's specially intimate friend was an elderly man who worked as accountant in some obscure commercial office in Southwark. Trink's closest friend was a shop-keeper; a man who kept what was called a "general" shop at the northern end of Talleyrand Street.

Mendel, despite his own assorted friendships, could never quite understand *that* friendship. The shop-keeper had no oddities, no character, no corner where he even grazed the amused observation of Trink. It may have been, of course—and this fact explains many ill-assorted friendships—that they liked the same kind of funny story, or walked at the same pace in the streets, or liked the same kind of food and drink. Friendships *are* bound by slender things like that. Or it may have been that they were bound by love. There must have been more in it than mere liking, or Trink, being what he was, could have found no pleasure in the pale copy-book talk of Timothy Reece. Mendel had seen them together, and had thought he could perceive on either side something almost of devotion. He had noted their content in long silence, when they merely sat and smoked, and their quick voiceless greeting when they met. Trink seemed to be happier with that mindless shop-keeper than with anybody.

Talleyrand Street makes part of a district of long, meaningless streets and disinherited houses. Once, those houses were the homes of the prosperous; now they cherish faded memories, and at night their faces are mournful and evocative. Fashion and prosperity have turned their backs upon them, and their walls enclose no stronger urge than furtive and shabby commerce. They lie, those streets and houses, in an uneasy coma, oppressed by a miasma of the second-hand and the out-moded—second-hand shops, second-hand goods, second-hand lodgings filled with second-hand furniture, and used by second-hand people breathing second-hand denatured air. They have not the cheerful acquiescence of the poor who have always been poor but the craven chill of the "come-down."

Talleyrand Street is just one of those streets, and when Reece set up his shop he blunderingly chose the apt setting for himself and his family. They belonged there. They were typical of a thousand decent, hard-working, but ineffectual families of our cities. For four genera-tions the family had not changed its social level. A faint desire to improve they may have had, but improving means adventure, and they feared adventure. On the wife's side and the husband's side the strain was the same—lukewarm and lackadaisical. There they had stood these many years, like rootless twigs in the waste patch between the stones and the pastures; and there, since the only alternative was risk and struggle, they were content to stand. Reece himself had the instincts of the aristocrat hidden in the habits of the peasant. One of life's misfits. He had the fine feature and clear eye of that type, but though he looked like what is called a gentleman, nobody would have taken him for one. His refinement of feature and manner came really, not from the breeding of pure strains, but from under nourish-ment in childhood.

His wife was largely of his sort. Her life had been a life of pain and trial, and it had taught her nothing. Her large, soft face was expressionless. The thousand experiences of life had left not even a finger-print there, and she still received the disappointments and blows of fortune with indignation and querulous collapse.

There were two boys and a girl. The girl had something of her father's physical refinement. Her head and face were beautiful; so beautiful that people turned to glance at her as she passed. Her manners and voice were—well, dreadful. She would often respond to those admiring glances by putting out her tongue. She was wholly unconscious of her beauty, not because she was less vain than her sex, but because her beauty was not to her own taste. She admired and envied girls of florid complexion and large blue eyes and masses of hair—chocolate-box beauties—and her own beauty was a glorious gift thrown to the dogs. To see that grave dark head and those deep Madonna eyes set against those sprawling manners and graceless talk gave one a shudder. It was like seeing a Sung vase set in the middle of a Woolworth store.

The two boys were two clods. They lived their lives in a kind of coma of eating, working and sleeping. They asked no more of the world than one long hebetude. One might say that they saw life as nothing but a programme of getting up, going to work, working, eating, going to bed. Only it wouldn't be true. They saw life no more than a three-months-old baby sees life. They were like millions of their fellow-organisms—deaf, dumb, torpid and myopic.

Those were the people Trink had chosen as special friends, and by all of them he was, not adored, for they were incapable of that, but liked to the fullest extent of their liking. He was their honoured guest, and on his side he gave to all of them affection and respect. As citizens they were entitled to respect, and they received it not only from him but from their neighbours. They had the agreeably-willing shop manners that customers like, and they maintained a constant goodwill. The two boys worked in a boot and shoe factory, and the shop was run by the Reeces and the girl, Olive.

Olive knew enough about the business to do her bit without any mental strain, and she had a flow of smiles and empty chatter that in such a shop was useful.

Those shops called "general" shops, often spoken of as Little Gold-Mines, are usually set, like that shop, in side-streets. It is by their isolated setting that they flourish. The main streets are not their territory. Their right place is a situation as far from the competition of the multiple stores as possible, and in the centre of a thicket. In that situation they win prosperity from the housewife's slips of memory.

So the Reeces were doing well. Indeed, they were very comfortable and could have been more than comfortable; but they were so inept, and knew so little of the art of useful spending, that their profits showed little effect in the home. If they could not be given the positive description of a happy family, at least they lived in that sluggish sympathy which characters only faintly aware of themselves give each other; and that was the feeling of the home—lymphatic and never *quite*. The wireless set worked, but it was never in perfect tone. The sitting-room fire would light, but only after it had been coaxed by those who knew its "ways". The hot-water in the bathroom was never more than very warm. The flowers in the garden were never completely and unmistakably blossoms. The shop door would shut, but only after three sharp pressures—the third a bad-tempered one. They bought expensive and warranted clocks, and the clocks took the note of the family and were never "right". New and better pieces of furniture were frequently added, and the rooms never succeeded in looking furnished. The colours did not harmonise nor did they scream. They made a grievous wail. Going one step beyond a good workman's dwelling, their home stopped short of even the poorest suburban villa.

Hardly a family, one would think, marked out for tragedy, or even disaster; yet it was upon those lustreless, half-living people that a fury of annihilation rushed from nowhere and fell, whirling them from obscurity and fixing their names and habits in the scarlet immortality of The Talleyrand Street Shop Murder.

It was about the time when those gangs called The Boys were getting too cocksure of their invulnerability, and were extending their attentions from rival gangs to the general public, that the catastrophe came by which Stephen Trink lost his one close friend. Beginning with small post offices, the gangs passed to little isolated shops. From all parts of London came reports of raids on those shops. The approach was almost a formula. "Give us a fiver. Come on. Gonna 'and over or d'ye want yer place smashed up?" Given that alternative the little shopkeeper could do nothing but pay. He might have refused, and have had his place smashed up, and he might have been able to get the police along in time to catch two or three of the gang and get them six or twelve months each. But that wouldn't have hurt them, since their brutal and perilous ways of life make them fearless; and he would still be left with a smashed shop, pounds' worth of damaged and unsaleable goods, the loss of three or four days' custom during repairs, and no hope of compensation. So, as a matter of commonsense, he paid up; and serious citizens wrote to the papers and asked if this was the so-called twentieth century, and how long would the public tolerate, etc.

Then, on top of those raids, came the murder of the Reeces.

Marvellous and impenetrable is the potency of words. By the measure and tone of certain syllables people are moved this way and that, they know not how; nor can those orators or poets who work upon them through these rhythms analyse the power by which they work. As numbers of illustrious men could not have lived the histories they did live, had they borne other names than those we know them by, so certain ideas press more profoundly upon our minds by the weight of the words in which man has clothed them.

There is a harmony between these words and their master-ideas, as between men's lives and their names; a poetic justice. You have the faint spirit-echo of Shelley; the cool Englishness of Shakespeare; the homespun strength of Bunyan; the massy crags of Ludwig von Beethoven. Speak the word Mozart and the word Wagner, and you perceive the personal essence of either man's work. Hector Berlioz could not have pursued his high-fevered career under the name of Georges Jourdain. Nathaniel Hawthorne could not have written the spectral prose he did write had his name been Harry Robinson. Frederic Chopin could not have written his Preludes under the name of Jules Burgomaster. Oliver Cromwell, Napoleon Buonaparte, Charlemagne, Chateaubriand—the syllables of those names are steeped in a distillation of essential hues by which the characters and complexions of their bearers were fore-ordained. And so with ideas; and so, particularly, with that idea for which our sign and sound is *Murder*.

It could not have been more aptly named. It carries a shade and tone not wholly due to our association of it with the fact for which it is the graph. It could not represent an act of courtesy, or a dinner-dish or a Spring flower. There is dread and profundity in its very cadence. You may cry aloud "Jones has killed John Brown!" and the message carries nothing of that echo from the dark corridors of the soul that arises against our inner ears with the utterance of the word Murder.

By long association, murder is linked in our minds with midnight, or at least with dark; and those two conceptions of the cloaked side of nature combine in dreadfulness to make deeper dread. But harmoniou combinations of dreadfulness, though they intensify each other, are dreadfulness only, and are therefore less potent to pluck at the heart than dreadfulness in discord with its setting; for *there* comes in the monstrous. Murder at midnight, though it will shock as it has shocked through centuries of civilisation, is a shock in its apt setting. But murder in sunlight is a thought that freezes and appals. It bares our souls to the satanic shudder of blood on primroses.

One can catch then the bitter savour of a certain moment of a sunny afternoon in Talleyrand Street. It was just after three o'clock of a September afternoon; a September of unusual heat. The heat made a blanket over the city, and in the side-streets life was in arrest, bound in slumber and steam and dust. In Talleyrand Street carts and cars stood outside shops and houses as though they would never move again. Even the shops had half-closed their eyes. Errand boys and workless labourers lounged or lay near the shops, sharing jealously every yard of the shade afforded by the shop-blinds. The faded Regency houses stewed and threw up a frowst. Through the dun length of the street the heat played in a fetid shimmer and shrouded either end in an illusion of infinity. The gritty odours of vegetable stalls, mixed with the acrid fumes of the cast-off clothes shops, were drawn up in the sun's path to float in the air and fret the noses of the loungers. The ice-cream cart, zoned with the Italian colours, made a cool centre for the idle young. A woman was offering chrysanthemums from a barrow piled high with that flower. Her barrow and her apron made a patch of living gold against the parched brown of the street.

Then, into this purring hour, came a figure and a voice. From the upper end of the street it came, crying one word; and the blunt syllables of that word went through the heat and dust, and struck the ears of those within hearing with the impact of cold iron. The street did not stir into life. It exploded.

Those nearest scrambled up, crying—not saying; such is the power of that word that it will always be answered with a cry—crying "Where? Where?" "In there—

three-ninety-two." And the man ran on to Mirabeau Street, still crying; and those who had heard the word ran in a trail to number 392.

The shop, with its battling odours of bacon, cheese, paraffin, spice, bread, pickles, was empty. The runners looked beyond it. A small door led from the shop to the back parlour. The upper half of the door was glass, and this half was veiled by a soiled lace curtain. Its purpose was to screen the folk in the parlour—where they sat at intervals between trade rushes—from the eyes of customers, while those in the parlour could, by the greater light of the shop, see all comers. But since the curtain served a purely workaday room—the real private sitting-room was upstairs—it had been allowed to over-serve its time, and frequent washings had left it with so many holes that its purpose was defeated. People in the shop could, by those holes, see straight and clearly into the parlour; could see the little desk with account-books and bills, and could often see the cash-box and safe, and hear the rattle of accountancy. It was proved by later experiment that a man on the threshold of the shop could, without peering, see what was going on in the shop-parlour.

The leaders of the crowd looked hastily about the shop and behind the two small counters; then, through those holes, they had the first glimpse of what they had come to see.

The sun was at the back. It shone through the garden window and made a blurred shaft of dancing motes across the worn carpet and across the body of Timothy Reece. He lay beside his desk. The back of his head was cleanly broken. By the door leading to the inner passage lay the body of Mrs. Reece. She lay with hands up, as though praying. Her head was flung violently back, disjointed. Of the two boys, who had been spending the last day of their holidays at home, the younger, Harold, lay in a corner by the window, almost in a sitting posture. His head hung sideways, showing a dark suffusion under the

left ear. The leaders looked and saw. Then someone
said—"The girl!"

They pulled open the door leading to passage and
kitchen. In the sun-flushed passage lay the twisted body
of Olive Reece. Her head, too, was thrown back in
contortion. One glance at the excoriations on her neck
told them how she had met her death. Three glances
told them of the dreadful group that must have made
entrance there; one to kill with a knife, one with a blow,
and one to strangle with the hands.

For some seconds those inside could not speak; but
as the crowd from the street pushed into the shop, and
those in the shop were pushed into the parlour, those
inside turned to push them back; and one of them,
finding voice, cried uselessly, as is the way in dark
moments, "Why? Why all this—these nice people—just
for a pound or two. It's—it's—*too silly*!"

He was right, and this was felt more strongly when it
was found that this thing had not been done for a pound
or two. The desk was locked, and the cash-box and
the two tills in the shop were intact. Clearly this was not
haphazard killing for robbery. There was a grotesquerie
about the scene that hinted at more than killing; an
afterthought of the devilish. Those people, who had
led their ignoble but decent lives in ignoble streets,
were made still more ignoble in death. The battered
head of Reece, the crumpled bulk of Mrs. Reece, the
macabre distortion of the symmetry of youth, were more
than death. The peace that touches the most ugly and
malign to dignity, the one moment of majesty that is
granted at last to us all, was denied them.

So they lay in the floating sunshine of that afternoon,
and so the crowd stood and stared down at them until
the police came. Who had done this thing? Where
were they? How did they do it in an open shop? How
did they get away? Why was it done?

Then someone who knew the family cried, "Where's
Percy?" And some went upstairs and some went into

the little garden. But all that they found was an open bedroom window and signs of a flight. No Percy.

It was between three and four o'clock of the day when Mendel had given himself that razor cut that Trink made one of his "drop-in" calls. Mendel was accustomed to those calls. Trink would come in, potter about, turn over any new books and periodicals, make a few remarks about nothing, disturb the atmosphere generally, and then slide away. But that afternoon, Mendel noticed, he didn't disturb the atmosphere. He seemed lighter and brighter than usual. Something of the morning mood in which Mendel had seen him seemed still to be with him. Tired and pale he certainly was— perhaps the result of a night walk—but Mendel noted a serenity that was both new and pleasing, and seeking a phrase could only find the crude phrase, "more human".

He stayed but a short time; not fidgeting but sitting restfully on the chesterfield as men do after long physical exercise. Mendel remarked on this; told him that he had seen him that morning sailing through the square; and told him that the sailing and his present mood proved that plenty of exercise was what he needed, and that he would no doubt find, as George Borrow found, that it was a potent agent for the conquest of accidie—or liver. He smiled; dismissed the diagnosis of his trouble, and soon afterwards faded away, so that when Mendel resumed work he was barely certain that Trink had been there at all. He never saw him again.

But about an hour later he was aware that he was disturbed, and when, half-consciously and still at work, he tried to analyse the disturbance, he located it as something coming from the street; a sound that came at first from below the afternoon din, then rose to its level and spilled over it. It was the cry of newspaper boys. The ear of the born Londoner is so adjusted that it can isolate street sounds from each other and perceive any dislocation or fine distinction from the normal; and though Mendel was still concentrated on his work, and could not hear a word the boys were crying, his ear told him of a dire intonation that did not belong to Winners and S.P. Before he even listened to the cry, he knew that they were crying news of some disaster, and became curious about it. So he went to the telephone, and rang a friend on the *Evening Mercury*, and asked what was the big story. The friend gave it so far as it had then come in.

His immediate thought on hearing the story was of what it would mean to Trink. He had known Reece only slightly, through Trink, and terrible as the fate of the family was, they meant nothing to him, and he could feel for them only the detached and fleeting pity that we feel at any reported disaster with which we are not concerned. But for Trink, their friend, it would be a blow, and a keener blow since it came with such precision on top of his happy swinging mood of that day. He had just, it seemed, found some respite from his customary gloom, only to be brutally flung back into it, and deeper. Mendel thought at first of going round to him, and then thought not. He would want no intruders. It is the instinct of those in pain, physical or mental, to hide, since pain is as great a social offence as poverty, and the cruellest insult we can make to the suffering is to recognise their sufferings and offer them sympathy. He decided to wait until Trink chose to come in.

During the next hour or so the papers were publishing rush extras, and as the news had withdrawn him from work, and he could not return to it, he went out, bought all three evening papers and sat in a tea-shop reading them. There was no doubt that the affair, following the large publicity and discussion given to the shop-raids, had stirred the Press and alarmed the public. He saw it on the faces of the home-going crowd and heard it reflected in the casual remarks of stranger to stranger in the tea-shop and around the bus-stops. All that evening and night the word Murder beat and fluttered about the streets and suburban avenues, and wherever it brushed it left a smear of disquiet.

Accustomed as great cities are to murder, and lightly, even flippantly, as they take all disturbances, the details of this one moved them. Clearly it was no ordinary murder of anger or revenge, or for the removal of inconvenient people for gain. How could those little people have offended? Who would want them out of the way? If it was the work of The Boys, it might be anybody's turn next. If it wasn't the work of The Boys, and The Boys had never been known to go to such extremes, then, said the Press, it must have been the work of wandering lunatics of gorilla's strength and ferocity. And if they were loose, nobody would be safe. Private houses and people in the streets would be wholly at the mercy of such fearless and furious creatures as these appeared to be. In the meantime, they *were* loose; even now, perhaps, prowling about and contemplating another stroke; sitting by your side in train or bus, or marking your shop or home for their next visit. They were loose, and while they were loose they spread their dreadful essence as no artist or prophet can hope to spread *his*. Scores of mothers from the streets about Talleyrand Street, hearing the news and seizing on the Press conjecture of lunatics, ran to schools in the district to meet their children.

Through all the thousand little streets of the near and far suburbs went the howl of the newsboy, and its virulent accents went tingling through the nerves of happy households. To people sitting late in their gardens, veiled from the world, came at twilight a sudden trembling and sweeping of the veil as the wandering Chorus stained the summer night with that word. It broke into the bedrooms of wakeful children, and into the study of the scholar, and into the sick-room and across quiet supper-tables; and wherever it fell it left a wound. The Press, having given the wound, went on to probe and exacerbate it with the minutiae of horror; ending with the disturbing advice to householders to see to their bolt, and fastenings that night. It was the Splash story of the day, and each paper had a narrative from neighbours and from those who were near the shop at the time of the crime's discovery. At late evening the story was this.

Percy Reece had been found and interviewed. He explained his absence by the regrettable fact that he had run away. The information he could give was of no help to those engaged on the case. As that day was the last day of his holidays he had, he said, been taking things easy, and after the midday dinner he had gone upstairs to lie down. He left his brother in the garden. His father and sister were in the shop parlour, and his mother was in the shop. From two o'clock to five o'clock was a slack time with them. Most of the business came before twelve, or from five o'clock to closing time; the afternoon brought mere straggles of custom.

He remembered lying down on his bed, with coat and waistcoat off, and remembered nothing more until he suddenly awoke and found himself, in his phrase, all of a sweat. His head and hands were wet. He jumped up from the bed and stood uncertainly for a few moments, thinking he was going to be ill. And well he might have been ill, seeing what foul force was then sweeping through the air of that little house. Out of the sunlight something from the dark corners had come creeping upon it, to charge its rooms with poison and to fire it with the black lightning of sudden death.

At the moment he awoke this creeping corruption must then have been in the house, and in its presence not even so thick and wooden an organism as his could have slept. By some old sense of forest forefathers we are made aware of such presences. We can perceive evil in our neighbourhood through every channel of perception; can even see it through the skin. The potency of its vapours, then, must have worked upon the skin and senses of this lad, as the potency of the unseen reptile works upon the nerves of birds, and he awoke because a protecting presence had called him to awake. It must have been that, and not a cry or a blow, that awoke him because he said that, during the few seconds when he stood half-awake and sweating, he heard his mother's voice in a conversational murmur.

It was some seconds after that that the sweat froze on his face at the sound of his father's voice in three plodding syllables—"Oh . . .My . . . God!" —and then of a noise such as a coalman makes when he drops an empty sack on the pavement. And then, almost simultaneously with the sack sound, he heard a little squeak that ended in a gurgle; and over-riding the gurgle one "Oh!" of horror—his mother's voice—and another soft thud; and before the thud an "Oh!" of surprise from his brother, and soft, choking noises of terror. And then silence. And then he heard two sharp clicks, as of opening and shutting a door; and then a moment's pause; and then swift feet on the stairs.

Had he had the courage to go down on his father's first cry, his courage, one may guess, would have been wasted. Hands would have been waiting for him, and he too would have ended on a gurgle. But if he had had the courage to wait before he fled until the figure or figures on the stairs had come high enough to give him one glimpse, he might have had a clue to one of the men that would have helped to the others. But he didn't wait. He bolted. He offered the reporters no feeble excuse of going to raise the alarm or get help. He said that those sounds and the sort of feeling in the house so affected him with their hint of some irresistible horror that he didn't think of anybody or anything—only of getting out.

Peering from his door, he said, just as the sound of the feet came, he could see part of the staircase, and the sunlight through the glazed door between shop-passage and garden threw a shadow, or it might have been two shadows, half-way up the stairs. He could hear heavy panting. In the moment of his looking, the shadow began to swell and to move. He saw no more. In awkward phrases (so one of the reports said) he tried to say that he felt in that shadow something more than assault ending in killing, he felt something for which he couldn't find a word. So, driven by he knew not what, and made, for the first time in his life, to hurry, he turned from that house of dusty sunshine and death to the open world of sky and shops and people. He bolted through the upper window, into the garden, and over the wall, and didn't stop or call for help till he was four or five streets away; at which point the increasing cry led to a pursuit and capture of him.

He made his confession sadly but without shame. He *knew*, he said, that it was all over; that he could be of no use; that they were all dead. But when they pressed him *how* he knew, he relapsed from that moment of assertion into his customary beef-like stupor, and they could get no more from him than a mechanical "I dunno. I just knew." He was detained for questioning, and it appeared later that the questioning had been severe. But though at first there was an edge of official and public suspicion of him, he was able to satisfy everybody that he knew nothing, and was allowed to go home to some friend of the family.

No weapons were found, no finger-prints, no useful footprints. Nor had any suspicious characters been seen hanging about; at least, none markedly suspicious to the district, in whose misty byways queer characters of a sort were a regular feature, and whose houses were accustomed to receiving at all hours travelling strangers. Taking it at first sight as gang work, the authorities, it was said, were pursuing enquiries in that direction; which meant that for the next few days all known members of all gangs were rounded up and questioned or kept under observation. Already, at that early hour, reports had come in of the detention of unpleasant characters at points on the roads out of London— Highgate, Ealing, Tooting. Communication had been made with all lunatic asylums in and near London, but none could report any escapes.

There, that evening, it was left. Next morning there were further details, but nothing pointing towards an arrest. From some of the details it was clear that the affair, if planned at all, had been most cunningly planned and timed, and swiftly done, since the people were seen alive five minutes before that cry had shocked the still street. The more likely conjecture, though, was that it was the impulsive act of a wandering gang. A woman volunteered that she had visited the shop just after three, and had been served by Mrs. Reece. Nobody else was in the shop. She left the shop and went a little way down the street to leave a message with a friend, and having left the message she re-passed Reece's shop, and saw a man whom she did not closely notice standing at the counter rattling some coins and calling "Shop!" Her own home was twelve doors from the shop. She had scarcely got indoors, and taken off her hat when she heard that cry. In the immediate instant of silence following it she heard a church clock strike the quarter-past. Another statement came from a man whose house backed on to the Reeces'. He was on a night-shift, and went on at four o'clock. By daily use he knew exactly how to time himself to reach his work punctually from his home, and he left home regularly at ten minutes past three. He was just finishing dressing, he said, when, happening to glance through the window he saw Mr. and Mrs. Reece in their shop-parlour fiddling with account-books. That was at nine minutes past three.

Of the people who were in the street at the time the alarm was given, none could say anything useful. Indeed, the result was only more confusion. Fifteen people who had been near the spot were asked—Who was the man who rushed from the shop giving that cry? None of them knew him. They were then asked—What was he like? Not one could make a clear answer. Eleven were so surprised that they didn't look at him. The other four—who, if they had looked at him, hadn't seen him but wouldn't admit it—gave four different descriptions. One saw a tall firmly-built man with red face. One saw a short man in a mackintosh. One saw a man in shirt and trousers only—obviously a confusion with the flying Percy. One saw a stout man in a grey suit and bowler hat.

It seemed fairly certain, though, that the man who gave that cry could not have been concerned in the affair, since two witnesses had seen members of the family alive within less than two minutes of the alarm; and it was held that wholesale slaughter could not have been accomplished in that time. The man who ran out must have been the man who had been seen by the woman standing there and shouting "Shop!" He had not come forward, but there might be many innocent explanations of that. He might have been a man of nervous type who had received such a shock from what he had seen that he wished to wipe out all association with the affair. Or he might have been a quiet, shy fellow who would hate to be mixed up in any sensational public affair. Having given the alarm, and having no useful information to offer beyond what the crowd saw for themselves, he might consider that he had done his duty.

Generally it was felt that it must have been the work of a gang—either a gang of thieves who were disturbed by the alarm before they could get at the cash, or, as some paper suggested, a drunken or drugged gang; and the gang must have entered by the back or somebody in the street would have seen them. People in the neighbourhood, getting hypnotised by the affair, began to remember certain happenings centring on the Reeces which they considered strange and significant in the light of what had happened. Queer visitors, letters by every post, sudden outgoings, late homecomings—all the scores of everyday family happenings which, when isolated and focused by tragedy and publicity, assume an air of the sinister and portentous. If

Mrs. Reece had gone out the day before in a new hat, they would have seen that as a possible clue.

Day by day the story mounted, and all fact that was thin was fortified by flagrant conjecture, and by "sidelights" and comparison with similar crimes. All of it led nowhere. A clue was being followed at Leicester. A broken and stained bicycle pump had been found behind the bath in the bathroom. Watch was being kept at the ports. Newspapers offered rewards to possible "splits" but none came forward to give their friends away. The Sunday papers carried a story hinting that certain news might be expected from Birmingham. The Monday papers ran Birmingham. But after two days all of them were proudly silent on Birmingham.

Thereafter public and Press interest declined. From being a Splash story it came to an ordinary column; then, from the main page, it passed to the secondary news page; then it fell to half a column, and at the end of three weeks it breathed its last in a paragraph.

In all that time Mendel had seen and heard nothing of Stephen Trink. He knew what he must be feeling about it, since he himself, though quite unwarrantably, had been moved by it. It meant little more to him than a news story; yet he passed those days in positive disquiet. Beyond the fact of having once or twice met the people, as friends of Trink, he had no interest in them. Yet whenever he thought about the affair, he suffered a chill, as though they did mean something to him; an entirely unreasonable chill which he could not shake off because common sense could not reach it.

Then, about a month after the affair had faded, he found among his post a letter from Trink. It was dated from Paris, and was an unusually long letter from one who scarcely ever wrote more than a post card. And a queer letter, though since it was from Trink that in itself was not queer. He read it at breakfast, and for some long time, an hour or more, he could not bring himself to put it down and face the day. When at last he did, he found work impossible. All that day and night he was haunted by a spectre of forbidden knowledge, and he went about his occasions perfunctorily, with a creeping of the flesh, as when one discovers a baby playing with a boiling kettle, or touches something furry in the dark. He knew then what it was that the boy Percy was trying to say. This was the letter:

"Dear Mendel,

"As we haven't met for some time I thought you might like a word from me. I've been here for a week or so, seeking a little change for jangled nerves. You understand. It was a dreadful business, and I didn't want to see anybody, especially friends. I'm here doing nothing and seeing nothing—just breathing. I suppose they've got no farther with it. Strange that people are so astonishingly clever in abstruse cases, and so often beaten by a simple case. But you know how often, in art, a subtle piece of work which the public imagines to have been achieved by laborious and delicate process, was in fact done with perfect ease. They all seem to have been misled by that matter of time. They assumed that that little time, for such a business, must imply a gang. No sound reason why it should, though. As William Nevison established an alibi by accomplishing the believed impossible in the seventeenth century—committing a crime at Gad's Hill in Kent one morning, and being seen at York at seven o'clock the same evening—so this man deceived public opinion. Four murders by different means had been accomplished in about two minutes. Therefore, said the public, it must have been a gang. But public opinion is always saying It Can't Be Done, and is always eating its words. What any one man can conceive, some other man can do. I'm satisfied that this was the work of one man, and I'll show you how he could have done it and how he could have got away. As to that, of course he got

away by running away. If you say that a running
man at such a moment would attract attention, well,
that is what he did. He was clever enough to know
that in successfully running away, it depends how you
run. He covered his appearance and his haste by
drawing the whole street's attention to himself. He
knew enough about things to know that his cry would
blind everybody. They might be looking, but they
wouldn't be seeing—as we know they weren't. All their
senses would gather to reinforce the sense of hearing.
As soon as he was round a corner he could slip his hat
in his pocket and put on a cap. Nothing makes a
sharper edge on the memory, or more effectually
changes a man's appearance, than the hat. Then he
could take off his coat, throw it over his arm, and go
back and join the crowd. It was no planned affair and
no gang affair. It was the work of a man momentarily
careless of results. Being careless, he made no mistakes.

"As to *how*—really very simple. It's just this—he
was a man of extraordinary swiftness of act and motion.
People don't seem to realise on what a slender thread
human life hangs—until they fall down two steps, or
receive a cricket ball in the neck, or slip on the soap
in the bath. A man can be killed with less trouble than
a rabbit or a hen. A pressure on a certain spot, or a
sharp flick on a point at the back of the neck, and it's
done. It could be done on the top of a bus, at Lord's,
or at the theatre, or in your own home. That man, as
I say, was swifter than most of us. He strolled into the
shop. Calling 'Shop!' he went to the parlour door.
There he met Reece. One movement. Mrs. Reece
would turn. Another movement. The girl was coming
through the door leading to the passage. Two steps
and another movement. The boy comes through the
garden to the shop. A fourth movement. And it was
done. A movement overhead. The other boy stirring.
He waits for him to come down. The boy doesn't
come. He hears the noise of his flight. Then he makes

his own by running full tilt into the faces of a score of people and crying his crime.

"As to why a man not a natural criminal or lunatic should have created this horror of destruction—that is not so easy. Before I can present what looks to me like a reasonable explanation, I must ask you to empty your mind of *your* reason and of that knowledge of human nature on which people base their judgment of human motive and human behaviour. It should never be said that people don't *do* these things because at some time or other some person does do those things. You must see it as clearly as one sees a new scientific idea— without reference to past knowledge or belief. This man *had* a motive for his wanton slaughter, but not a motive that would pass with common understanding. Neither hate nor lust nor the morbid vanity that sometimes leads stupid people to the committal of enormous crimes. Nothing of that sort. And he wasn't a madman without responsibility for his actions. He knew what he was doing. He committed more than a crime. He committed a sin. And meant to. Most men think that sin is the ultimate depth to which man can sink, but this man didn't sink. He rose, by active sin, out of something darker than sin. That something is the spirit of unexpressed, *potential* evil; something that corrodes not only the soul of the man in whom it dwells, but the beautiful world about him. This evil doesn't always, indeed, seldom does, live in what we call wicked people. It lives almost always in the good, and in comparison with them the positive wicked are almost healthy. For these good people are germ-carriers and are more dangerous than criminals or sinners. They can penetrate everywhere. We have no armour against their miasma. They do no evil, but they are hives of evil. They lead stainless lives. Their talk is pure. Yet wherever they go they leave a trail that pollutes the nobility and honesty of others. They diffuse evil as some lonely country places, themselves beautiful, diffuse evil. Happy for them, poor creatures, if they can discover and prove themselves before death for what they are. Some do. They are lucky. There's something in these people. Some awful karma from the world's beginning. Some possession that can only be cast out in one way—a dreadful way. Where it began one cannot say. Perhaps some nightmare sins, projected in the hearts of creatures centuries-dead, projected but never given substance, take on a ghost-essence and wander through the hearts of men as cells of evil. And wander from heart to heart, poisoning as they go until at last they come to life in a positive sin, and, having lived, can die. Nobody knows. But that's my explanation of those people. They're possessed. An incubus sits upon them, and they can only be rid of it by some active sin. They must express and release that clotted evil, and they cannot be cleansed of it before it's expressed, as a man cannot be cleansed of a fever before it's reached its climacteric. Once expressed, it can be met and punished. But abstract evil can't be met.

"Let's suppose that this man was one of these, consciously possessed of this intangible essence of evil, conscious of it as a blight upon him and those around him; tortured by it like a man with a snake in his bosom, and fighting its desire for expression and release until the fight became intolerable. There's only one way of escape for him—to sin and to sin deeply. Always he fights the temptation, and so, continuing to shelter the evil, he gives it time to grow and to make his own emanations stronger. But his only real hope of killing it lies in giving it life.

"And then at last he yields. There comes, one day, the eruptive, whirlwind moment of temptation, stronger than any he has known. All his powers of resistance go down in an avalanche. With a sigh of relief he yields. And then, with the disappearance of resistance, and with the resolve to sin, he would find, I think, the serenity of resignation filling his whole being. And when the thing was done, the sin committed, the most dreadful sin he could conceive, in that Satanic moment he frees himself for ever from his incubus, not by binding it but by releasing it. Like a long-embalmed body exposed to the air, it has one minute of life, and the next it crumbles into dust and he is free.

"By that sin he can now, as a fulfilled and erring soul, work out his penance and his redemption. That's all."

THE MESSAGE OF CHAN-HSU-TSIANAH

IN the little room at the back of his store, which held all the aromatic odours that go into the most exotic Parisian perfumes, Old Quong set aside the chessboard, put his water-pipe on the table, and looked at me with as much expression of no-favour as an Eastern face ever holds.

And now (he said) I suppose you expect me to tell you a story. You always do. Am I a newspaper? But your recent remark about the affair at the Regalia Hotel in your city causes me to reflect upon certain aspects of human nature peculiar to certain human types.

One of your English poets—I forget which: to me their mewings sound so much alike—but one of them has said that simple faith is of greater worth than Norman blood. I do not know how it is possible to correlate such incongruous matters as a physical fluid and a moral attitude, and deduce their respective worth. But then, the intellectual caprices of your poets have always left me dismayed, and sometimes alarmed. Let it pass. He did say it. He did find something praiseworthy in simple faith. Which is more than I çan, and more than the great Buddha could.

But perhaps, from his observation of a certain section of the English people, he had cause. Perhaps, indeed, he only praised it because it is a feature of that section which all your English writers love to praise—that small section that was educated at the right schools, and sometimes buys books. For truly I have noted that of all English classes, the simple are the most hard to dazzle; while the wealthy, the privileged, and the sophisticated . . . Have you noted that those ingenious gentlemen who live by the performance of what you call The Confidence Trick never attempt to work it upon a simple rustic who has just sold his father's farm and is carrying the proceeds with him? Have you noted that the gentlemen you call Share-Pushers never waste their time in trying to extract the life-savings of simple working-people? No. For the Confidence Trick, they choose the wide, hard-headed business-man. And for the sale of worthless shares they choose the maiden lady of some education, the shrewd churchman, the alert sons of your prosperous middle-class. And they choose well. For, as one of my countrymen said—I think it was the far-seeing Weh-ti-li—if you want the true simpleton, you must look for him among the sons of guile.

But these are idle reflections, extraneous to your request for a story. Let us turn to matters of a less philosophic and less squalid nature; something quite remote from such things. Let me tell you the dramatic story of Chan-hsu-Tsianah.

His name to-day is not much known, but there was a time when he made quite a striking figure in the London scene. He was, as his name conveys, a countryman of mine, though from a different province, which means that had we spoken we should not have understood each other. I first heard of him at a time when many of the best minds in English intellectual life were turning for illumination to the East. It seems that he had arrived quietly in London without word of his coming; but however quietly a striking personage may arrive in London, your newspapers are bound to hear of it and to do all that they can to prevent his being quiet, while announcing his desire to be quiet. They are like those devoted wives who nurse their husbands' headaches by calling upstairs every ten minutes and telling them of the twenty different ways of relaxing.

It was said that he had come to London because he regarded it as the centre of the world, and the spot best suited for what he had to do. And what he had to do was to deliver a message that would release mankind and this age from all its pressing problems. Much as the newspapers pursued him, their representatives were unable to interview him. One or two caught a glimpse of him through an open door, seated on a rug in profound meditation; but his secretary refused to allow them any intercourse. From time to time she gave them some details of his daily life and habits, and stories of his long sojourn on the plateaux of Tibet; and with these they had to be content. No disclosure of the nature of the message could be given to them; nor could Chan-hsu-Tsianah say when he would deliver it. He was awaiting the right astrological minute.

Soon after his arrival he became a topic among all classes. One point made him a constant theme of the best dinner-tables. This was—that nobody knew how to pronounce his name, and the difference of opinion led to much discord. Many a social group was split by the secession of its members to one of the three opposed schools of thought. One school held the pronunciation to be Shan-see-Hwana. Another school stood for Hahn-hoo-zanna. While a third stood for San-zu-China. In one or two houses, so report said, regrettable scenes occurred. There was the case of the Duchess, firm San-zu-China fan, who hurled a full plate of bouillabaisse at the wife of the financier with whom the Duke was hoping to do business; all because the financier's wife had timidly suggested that perhaps the name was pronounced as spelt. There was the case of Mrs. Ponderby-Looping, who had to fly to Paris for a completely new face-treatment after trying to maintain Hahn-hoo-zanna against a Shan-see-Hwana adherent. And literary sherry-parties, I was told, became almost as noisy as parish meetings.

Some of the leading hostesses of London, and many who were bringing up the rear, wracked what they would have called their brains to devise means of being the first to—I think you call it—Take Him Up. But he would not be Taken Up. He lived in silence, seclusion, and austerity, in frequently changed lodgings. Sometimes he was in that nether-world of splendour, Cromwell Road; sometimes in the arctic glory of Bayswater; and for one period he sought the quiet severity of Camden Town. He would take no part in what he described as the ungainly mummery of the social world. Hostesses pestered their husbands to discover what sort of bribe could be offered to a man who had spent most of his life looking at nothing on uncomfortable mountain-crags. But nobody could enlighten them. Money could mean nothing to a man who wore one robe, ate one square of bean-cake a day, and had attained the point of the cessation of all desire. One of them did, I believe, try the offer of building a Temple for him in the nicest part of Pentonville Road, where her husband owned a vacant site that wouldn't sell. When this failed, they gave it up.

The newspapers continued to write stories about him, and common people continued to talk about him. But the social world became occupied by the messages delivered so readily by a female film-star, a female skating-star, and a new and debonair ambassador; and for a time it forgot the promised message of Chan-hsu-Tsianah. It was recalled to some shadow of its former enthusiasm by an announcement in all papers that he had chosen a certain day of June for the delivery of his message. Not, Society was glad to see, Derby Day. It was to be delivered at the Spinoza Hall at nine o'clock in the evening of the chosen day. The seating accommodation of the Spinoza Hall was five hundred, and tickets would be limited to that number. Tickets were to be had at one guinea each.

The message, when at last it was delivered, created a profound stir. Those who did not go were, for some time, very much out of things. Those who were fortunate enough to secure tickets went about with the air of having been initiated, and greeted each other with reserved signals. What effect it had in bringing their lives into harmony with the eternal, I never heard, but I did hear that it gave them something of that quietness which is postulated as the essential of true change.

When the date of its delivery was announced, enthusiasm, as I have said, had waned. But it quickly recovered. Nobody liked to say they were not interested, in case that wasn't being said. Fearing that everybody else would be buying tickets, they all bought them. All those who could, because in two days the hall was sold out.

The gathering, so I was told by a trustworthy informant, was most distinguished. It was, indeed, a typical West End audience. It represented all that is most vociferous and most photographed in English life; and its puzzled look, as of a camel walking on hard pavement, made clear to Chan-hsu-Tsianah all that had ever confused him about the English. Small glasses of sherbet, and little bowls of rice, were offered to the distinguished company, and the distinguished company took them solemnly, and solemnly swallowed them.

When Chan-hsu-Tsianah had announced his message for nine o'clock, he had allowed (no doubt by prompting from his secretary) for that courtesy which is so marked in the best English society; that courtesy by which, for fear of embarrassing the management of a hall or theatre, they never arrive until half an hour after the appointed time. So that it was at ten o'clock that the yellow curtain of the platform was withdrawn, and the venerable Chan-hsu-Tsianah was seen by the privileged five hundred. He stood there in his one simple robe—such a robe as a commercial traveller might wear as a dressing-gown in commercial hotels—and gazed upon them. When they had taken their fill of gazing upon him, they noticed that the only other object on the platform was a large easel bearing a large blackboard.

The company slowly rustled into complete silence, and when this was accomplished, Chan-hsu-Tsianah raised his left hand to the level of his head, palm outward, and went with measured step to the blackboard.

Very gently, the yellow curtain glided along until it covered him. For some thirty or forty seconds, the audience sat tense and expectant. Each member could feel something in the air; some vibration from that aloof and venerable figure; some current of emotion that gave to each and all such a thrill of suspense as they had seldom enjoyed. Then the yellow curtain glided back, and they unbound their muscles, and their pulses resumed their function.

It was not (Old Quong continued) until the morning of the day when the message was to be delivered that I learned that Chan-hsu-Tsianah had been living for some years in this quarter—indeed, in this very street, a few doors away; but under his own name, which wasn't Chan-hsu-Tsianah. And that his manager in this matter was an interesting character of this quarter, known as Young Fred. Young Fred was a youth whose moral principles were ten a penny, and who spent much of his time in the invention of all kinds of methods for increasing your income in your spare time or any time. It was from him that I gathered all that I have just passed to you.

When I gathered that *he* was the business manager of Chan-hsu-Tsianah, I need hardly add that I was not surprised when he told me that the withdrawn curtain revealed an empty platform, and that the blackboard bore the message:

Home, you pie-cans, and I hope it keeps fine for you.

ESTELLA AND DOLORES

THAT part of Bayswater which calls itself North Kensington, just before it goes west (in two senses) and loses itself in the bleak but crowded mists of Notting Dale, has many recesses and labyrinths unguessed by those who use only the main roads. Those streets and terraces and arbours are mainly lined with large houses in the stucco of the Regency, though here and there are little lanes of cottages of an earlier date, some with an aspect that candour could only call genteel, others as rakishly down-at-heel as the illustrated papers in a dentist's waiting-room.

Hugo Floom, the white-haired, ex-professor of philosophy and habitual noctambulist, often pursued his hobby of night-wandering in this quarter, sometimes finishing in the last uncharted reaches of Harrow Road and sometimes amid the wastes of Wormwood Scrubs. On a certain dark, damp night, he had been wandering in that triangle made by Westbourne Grove, Ladbroke Grove and the canal, and had passed through a street of neat shops and branch banks and estate offices, and had made two turns from it, and found himself in one of the little lanes. It was one of the shabbier sort, and at about its middle was some kind of hall—a parish hall or mission hall—where a disturbed meeting seemed to be going on. Floom at once went towards it. A meeting always attracted him, since it often helped him in his study of the complicated life of the metropolis by throwing light on the doings of his fellow creatures.

When he entered the hall, he found a company of about twenty or thirty. With the exception of two girls and a gaunt man with a black beard, who seemed, like himself, to have "looked in," they appeared to be rowdies from the street. Their purpose seemed to be to break up the meeting; there was stamping of boots, whistles, cat-calls, and song choruses. The little platform held one man, who was trying to conduct the meeting, and in the front row a thick-set man was finishing a speech. Floom caught only the last few words, and tried to calculate how many times in his life he had heard that identical peroration:

"——and so, friends—go forward—stand together—forces of our opponents powerless against right and unity. The dawn—the battle—our goal——"

The rest was unheard through the stamps and howls of the audience. The speaker sat down, and after a moment got up and went into an ante-room just by the platform. Floom moved down the hall amid the uproar and took a seat in the third row of chairs, next to one of the girls—a pale girl with black hair in braids about her ears. As he sat down, he noted, just below the uproar, a continuous buzzing and intermittent thudding from the ante-room.

The chairman, a lean young man with sharp face and too-open eyes, was making feeble protests, when the man with the black beard, who was sitting in front of Floom next to a demure and petite blonde, stood up and lifted a large hand and a thin voice:—

"Mr. Chairman. A thought!"

At sight of this, the chairman wagged his head wearily, and his murmur, in a Notting Dale voice, could be heard where Floom was sitting: "'Strewth, not *again*?" Some sort of signal passed from him to the blonde girl, and Floom noticed that she acknowledged it with a nod. The bearded man went on. "A thought. May we not compare your movement to a river?"

A fruity voice from behind yelled: "Why should we, mate?"

The bearded man ignored the voice. "Just as the river receives tributaries, and is linked with other rivers by canals, so you——"

The chairman rose. Apparently he had not had many lessons in public speaking or voice production. "I don' think our friend's quite got the 'ang of the subjick and purpose of our meeting."

The fruity voice broke in. "No—nor nobody else neither. I bin listening half an hour, and damn-all I can make out of what you're here for. What *are* yer for?"

His comrades supported him with stamping feet and a roared chorus: "Yerce—what *are* yer for?"

"Our purpose," said the chairman, consulting a slip of paper, "is—er—co-ordination and direction."

"Yerce, but where to?" The rest joined in. "That's right—where to?"

"It's reely the abstrack we're dealing with."

"I should damn well think so. And what *is* the abstrack?" The crowd again joined in. "Yerce, what is the abstrack? We'd like to know. Is it in the Zoo?"

"It's a kind of—ah. But come now—order! The lady in the third row has something to say."

The girl next to Floom stood up, and he noted that her face had a graceful contour, but was spoiled by somewhat hard eyes and mouth. She was greeted with ignoble comments and crude noises. She ignored them. She took up some point made by the speaker whose peroration he had heard, and she quoted Kelvin on dynamics, Woodberry on Emerson, Petrie on Egypt, Galton on eugenics, Sharp on folk songs and Carlyle on Frederick the Great. From this, Floom deduced that she had been reading herself to sleep with the volume— "DYN-FRE"—of some encyclopaedia; which perhaps accounted for the hard eyes and mouth. As she finished, the chairman made the kind of signal he had made to the other girl, and as she sat down she gave a quick nod. At the same moment, a square-jawed young man, in a very Mayfair suit and Mayfair hairdressing, came from the ante-room, and sat in the front row, near its door.

The chairman congratulated the girl on what he called her real peach of a speech, which brought a volley

of stamps and meows from the audience, and then called
upon the Mayfair young man.

The Mayfair man spoke for some minutes, through
whistles and yells, and his speech seemed to Floom
strangely reminiscent of three articles in that morning's
Daily Messenger, on the need for a national theatre, on
the need for a vigorous agricultural policy, and on the
waste of money in social services. Floom was not dismayed; he had heard speeches like these at far more
august functions. The moment the Mayfair man sat
down the bearded man was again on his feet. "Mr.
Chairman, a thought!" (The chairman put his face in
his hands and murmured, "'Ow long, O Lord, 'ow
long?") "A thought. Could we not say that life is
like a theatre?"

The fruity voice assured him, "Yerce, we could *not*."

"There are seats for all of us in our degree."

"Why not take one, and keep it?"

"We could carry the figure farther——"

"And we will if yuh don't sit down. It's only 'alf a
mile to the canal."

"One might say——"

Floom lost the rest of it. His attention was distracted
by the sight of a little white patch on his knee. He
saw that it was a folded note. He opened it, and found
a pencil scrawl. "I am in great danger. Will you help
me? If so, go out. I will follow." He turned to the girl
at his side, and a faint movement of her mouth told him
that it was from her. He nodded, and inwardly rejoiced.
Here was adventure of some sort, if only of gallantry.
So, after allowing a minute's interval, in case their
glances had been noted, he got up with an air of bored
detachment, and went slowly and casually to the door,
and into the narrow street.

He turned and walked a few paces from the hall, and
waited. Within two minutes he heard a light step behind
him. He turned and raised his hat. "And in what way,
young lady, can I be of service?" As he turned, he saw

the bearded man come from the hall with the little blonde girl, and accompany her, with a more than fatherly air, towards the other end of the street.

"You could be the means of saving my life," the dark girl said. "That is, if you think it worth saving."

"Beauty is so scarce that it's always worth saving."

"Perhaps if you knew all—— But there, you look so kind and venerable that I'm sure you would not only give help but pardon as well."

"It is scarcely for one human creature to pardon another. We're all in need of it. But you speak of saving your life. Surely you're not in that kind of danger—in the middle of modern London?"

"I assure you I am."

"But how? Who's threatening you?"

She lifted a slender arm from under her cloak and pointed down the street with the precision of one aiming a revolver. She pointed to the other couple who were walking slowly away. "That man!"

Floom frowned. "*That* man? That woolly-minded old fuss-pot? Surely you're not—— Surely he couldn't."

"Ah, you judge by appearances. So, at one time, did I. It's part of the disguise under which he does his dreadful work. Nobody thinks him capable of anything— except losing trains or forgetting his latchkey. And yet, actually, he's capable of such things—and has done such things—that I could hardly mention them."

"Such things as what?" Floom, whose mind had some odd corners, hoped she would mention them; in the odd corners were fluttering certain scarlet images of palaces in the mountains of Cathay and of dens in the Baghdad of Haroun-al-Raschid.

She did mention them. As they stood in the dreaming mist of that everyday London by-street she told him a tale that made him see the bearded man, whom he had thought an old woman, as something devilish; the more devilish because of his ordinary appearance and fussy behaviour. Devilry from a devilish man is never so dreadful as devilry from a sleek and respectable citizen. He listened with horrified attention, and then asked: "And what do you want me to do?"

"Help me to escape."

"But where could I take you?"

"I don't want you to take me anywhere." (He had a moment's disappointment.) "I want you to help me in another way. For two years, since I first trusted myself to him, I've suffered so much that I reached the point of not caring. But to-day I made a resolution, and to-night, with your help, I'm going where he'll never find me. Don't ask me where. I have a friend who's going there, and is willing to take me, and it's a place that not even that man would think of. He'd think of Paris, or America, or the Mediterranean, but not this place. But there's no time to lose. See, he's looking this way."

Floom turned and saw the man and the blonde girl with heads bent in their direction. "If he suspected anything, and overtook me, he'd—he'd kill me. I know too much for him to let me live away from him. You *will* help, won't you."

Floom was emphatic. "In any way I can."

"Thank you. Then what I want you to do is to keep him engaged in some way until eleven. After that, I shall be gone. Keep close to him and keep him away from railway stations. That's all. At eleven o'clock you can drop him and go home. And you will know that you've been of great service to one who'll never forget it."

Before she had spoken her last words, Floom broke in. "You can count on me, young lady. I've sometimes been called the biggest bore in London."

"Surely not. With your distinguished——"

"Yes. It's been said that once I start talking, nobody can escape me. I'll see to it that that man doesn't."

The girl took his hand and pressed it. "God bless you."

He waved divine grace aside. "Oh, not at all. To be able to help so charming a lady, to get you away from that beast, will be its own reward. But may I not know whom I'm helping?"

"Better not. Remember only that you've saved the life of—well, my Christian name is Estella. And now—thank you again and good night." And with a quick, sad smile she was gone.

As he turned to take up his duty, he saw that the blonde girl had disappeared, and that the bearded man was just turning the corner of the street. He hurried after him, turned the corner, and found that instead of, as he imagined, wishing to avoid him, the man appeared to be waiting for him. The thin voice greeted him. "Good evening, sir. An interesting meeting, don't you think?"

Floom nodded. "Interesting in a way. But scarcely conclusive."

"Meetings seldom are. Which way are you going?" The man looked intently at him, and then up and down the street.

"Any way suits me," Floom said, and moved closer to him.

"Indeed? Excellent. Then let us stroll to the main road. I thought that young girl made a profound little talk."

"Who? Es—— Oh, the dark girl. Yes, but a little confused."

"The female mind often is. But stay, a thought! Here's a quiet little public house. I don't know whether you ever——"

"I do. As professor of philosophy I find that truth may as often be found at the bottom of a tankard as at the bottom of——"

"As a professor of——?"

"Philosophy."

The bearded man gave a short laugh. "Indeed! But, of course, now that I look, I see that you have, if I may be personal, something of that air. It sits well on you. But let us go in."

The bar into which he led Floom was neither little nor quiet. It was large and full, and so modern in decoration that Floom looked round in apprehension that at any moment he might be assaulted by the braying of a dance band. They sat down by a fireplace that had on its shelf one of those magnificent gilt and marble presentation clocks which, like all magnificent presentation clocks, wherever you find them, was out of order. By some means the bearded man got Floom to the wall seat of the table, and wedged it against him, and himself sat with his back to the door. Then, as soon as their drinks were served, he leaned across the table, and the black beard began wagging under Floom's nose. He spoke in a murmur.

"Sir—or professor of philosophy as you style yourself—I know that I'm placing myself in grave danger with you. But as a citizen, I put duty before personal safety. You may be able to damage me, and other people in this place. But whatever happens to me, you will never deliver those papers."

"Papers?" Floom's brow lifted in surprise, and fell in a frown. "What on earth are you talking about?"

"About you, sir. Ha! You thought yourself safe. But, alas, you've been given away."

"Given away? Me? Are you mad, sir? Or drunk?"

"Neither, sir. Acting on what I know of you, I brought you here because I could not see a policeman in the street, and you might have got away from me. You can't get away from here. There are plenty of men who would stop you. But I don't, if possible, want to be mixed up in any ugly, public brawl. So it will be sufficient if you thrust those papers into that fire there, unopened."

"I haven't the least idea what you're referring to."

"It's useless to bluff, sir. When I say papers I mean that sealed packet of instructions which you're carrying to headquarters."

"Headquarters of what?"

"The I.R.A., of course."

Floom laughed, and the bearded man glared. "It's no laughing matter, sir."

"Madness never is. And certainly you're mad. But from what I've heard of your life I don't wonder."

"My life, sir? And what should you know of my life?"

"I know a great deal."

"There is nothing in my life that can interest anybody. But Dolores has told me all about *yours*."

"Dolores? Who on earth is Dolores?"

"You affect ignorance and surprise very well, sir. But I suppose in your nefarious and shifty life it's necessary. But it gets nowhere with me. No, sir. Dolores is tired of the life of conspiracy, and after handing you those papers, she told me the story. It was a clever idea to make a rendezvous at a public meeting. It was not so clever of your chiefs to use a female as an emissary. They're so uncertain."

Floom put a flat hand on the table. "Listen to me, sir. I don't know what you're talking about, or why you invented this fantastic story about Dolores and sealed papers and I.R.A. I suppose you have some object of your own. But I have nothing to do with any Dolores or any sealed papers. Perhaps you will tell me what description you've invented for this Dolores?"

"I invented nothing, sir. She told me her name was Dolores. I mean the girl who sat next me in the hall."

Floom laughed again. "I never saw her before this evening. Your whole story is preposterous—a cover, I suppose, to your fears for yourself. You can make no charge against me to the police. But I can make one or two about *you*."

"About me? How dare you! But there, it's a common trick of the cornered man to accuse his accusers. I am certain you have those papers on you. I saw you, in the hall, out of the corner of my eye, put a paper in your pocket."

"You did, sir. It was an appeal for help against a villain. Against you, sir."

"Bluffing again? But I know more than you think. I know your address. I know where you're hoping to go with those papers. Dolores told me all your story."

"And I, sir, have *your* story—and a foul story it is—from Estella."

"Who?"

"Now who's bluffing? From Estella."

"I know no person of that name."

"The girl I sat next to in the hall. But she's out of your clutches now. You'll never see her again."

"I never saw her in my life till this evening. I have no female acquaintance at all."

"Really, sir. In face of what I know, you sit there and tell me that lie?"

"And you, in face of what *I* know, tell me you are not in league with the young person, Dolores?"

For two or three seconds they sat and glared at each other. Then Floom, noting the dithering anger of the bearded man, began to doubt. And the bearded man, noting Floom's flushed face and dignified resentment, also began to doubt. They held each other's eyes.

Then, simultaneously, they broke into speech, with a duet of "Do you swear, sir——?" They stopped, and began again, like two people trying to make way for each other in the street and making the same movement. "Do you sw——"

Then Floom said: "Pardon. Pray go on."

"I ask you," the other said, "do you swear that you carry no treasonous papers?"

Floom met him eye to eye, and said, "I swear it. I would, in another place, permit myself to be searched. I swear also that I have never till this evening seen or heard of the girl called Dolores."

The bearded man wagged his beard.

"Sir, I believe you. And in my turn I swear that I have never till this evening seen or heard of that young person who made the speech. And that my quiet and uninteresting life is open to any inspection."

They looked blankly at each other. Then Floom said: "I think we might as well drink our beer." They did. "But assuming we're both telling the truth, why should those girls have——?"

Up went the hand. "A thought! Things are not always what they seem. I believe that meeting was 'packed.' They wanted to get rid of us so as to carry some resolution without dissent."

"It didn't sound like it."

"No. But the other intruders didn't matter. They were merely rowdies. We were the only two who represented what could have been intelligent opposition."

Floom gave a sad smile. "*What* kind of opposition?"

"I begin to suspect something more than a packed meeting. Let us go back to that hall. At once."

They got up and went out. They hurried back the way they had come. As they reached the little street where the hall stood, the bearded man said, "Ha! Look!" A large touring car was just moving away. At the wheel Floom saw the sharp-faced chairman and next him the sleek-haired Mayfair boy. Behind, he saw the dark braids of "Estella" and the blonde head of "Dolores."

As it moved away, "Estella" looked over the back. She waved to Floom. "Thanks, darling, for keeping old Whiskers out of the way. Bye-bye." The blonde girl leaned out and cried to the bearded man: "Thanks, Landru, for looking after old Snowball."

The car shot away into the mist, and they stood looking after it. Then the bearded man raised a hand, but before he could say anything Floom broke in.

"Sir, if you're going to have another thought I shall feel inclined to kill you. It's quite clear that we've been *used*. Used against each other to cover some nefarious doings. I don't feel that we need have any thoughts about it."

"No. But *what* have they been doing? We ought to find out. A thought comes to me—I can't help it. Those noises going on in the ante-room—that stamping of feet and uproar which the chairman didn't attempt to check—because it drowned other noises. That meeting wasn't a meeting. The speakers were confederates, and those rowdies, I feel sure, were hired. Let us go inside."

The hall was still lit, but empty. They went through it to the ante-room, and there they saw two or three picks and drills. They saw also a pile of bricks and plaster and dust, and in the wall a large gaping hole leading into the building that backed on to the hall. The bearded man looked at it.

"Now what building backs on to this place? Ha! I remember, a branch of the Plutonian Bank. Dear, dear. If we'd only been a little more alert, if only I'd had a thought about those noises, we might have prevented a bank robbery."

Floom looked sour. He was thinking that here was another little adventure that would not bear telling. "Who cares? No bank's ever done anything for me. But being made a fool of. . . . Still, a nice girl, that Estella. Such a vivid imagination in fastening it on to—" (he looked the bearded man up and down) "—you. A pleasant companion for a little dinner, I should think. And I shall never——"

"So," said the bearded man, "was Dolores. In spite of her ridiculous slander in turning *you* into a desperado. We might say, don't you think, that life is like the ocean. Ships that pass in the——"

"Oh, shut up!"

MYSTERIOUS DISAPPEARANCE

"AND this job," said Young Fred in his high-pitched voice, "I'm going to do meself."

Young Fred and his boys were in conference in his dim and dusty home near the Regent's Canal corner of London. Young Fred was known in that corner for his industrious application to all means of increasing your income so long as those means did not involve work. His boys—the lanky Wally, the fat Barney, and the shrimp-like Spiv—were noted for doing all the work young Fred told them to do. However arduous it was, they did it gladly. Even when it was exhausting they found it more interesting than the work he often offered to get for them by his influence in certain quarters. So when he announced his decision to do a bit of work himself, they were suitably impressed. The fifth member of the group, Flaming Florrie, was not impressed.

"You better leave it alone, Fred. You'll only make a muck of it. Let one o' the boys do it. You never was good at action—not downstairs or upstairs."

Young Fred looked at her, and was going to squeak something, but he caught her eye and didn't. Flaming Florrie's name expressed her. Her height, her brassy hair, and her long swift arms added whatever confirmation was necessary to the name. Few men were any happier for knowing her. Most of them discovered this in seven days. Young Fred, who was a little slow in matters outside his business, had had four weeks of the company of Flaming Florrie, and was only aware that life had become a left foot in a right-hand-boot affair. It took him four more weeks to discover why.

But in spite of her threatening head and her swift arm, he remained firm on the subject of the conference. "No. I'll do it meself."

Florrie glared. "All right. Just when we want the doings, and have a chance of getting 'em, you go and let us down. Do it then, and I hope you're put away for it."

"Then you'll be disappointed," he squeaked. "I know the district, and I know the house. Barney's had it under observation the last fortnight, and it's a gift. The old chap collects his rents Monday morning and afternoon, and then goes home and has a lay-down. It's as easy as kiss-yer-hand. It ain't a job for Spiv or Wally. They ain't used to daylight jobs—though daylight's always easier, since at night everything's locked up, and in the day-time it's all open. You leave it to me. I'll do it quick and clean."

Florrie gave him a long expressionless look. "I bet yuh will. You're the Last of the Great Scouts, ain't yuh? You're Buffalo Bill and Sitting Bull and Red Eagle and Grey Owl. You was going to get the Phillibrass Castle stuff off old Suey Lim, and what did you get? A stiff. You and Wally was going to crack The Mint, and give us all a week-end at Brighton out of it, and you come back with one-and-tuppence—and you only got that by pressing Button B in telephone-boxes. You're the Great Noise, ain't yuh? Though you look to me more like the Last Trump."

Young Fred said nothing to this. It was not only wisdom that kept him silent, but lack of material for retort. He turned instead to his boys. "Spiv and Wally better come with me, in case I want to make a quick plant of the stuff. And they can keep look-out. You, Barney, you can stay and cheer Florrie up until I get back."

Florrie sighed. "What a Pleasant Monday Afternoon."

"I'll be back by six, and then I reckon we'll be set up for a week or two. Perhaps you and her can think up something new between yuh."

Florrie's face went more sour. "Last time Barney had

an idea was three Pancake Days ago. And then it fell out o' the pan, all wet."

"Well, anyway, you wait here till six o'clock, and then you'll see. It's time we were off. It's about half an hour from here to Ilford."

"All right. But it's so long since you did a job I'll be surprised if yuh do come back. Not sorry—just surprised."

Young Fred got up and took his hat. He wore a neat lounge suit and soft collar and tie. Though neat, the suit was shabby and inconspicuous; the kind of suit in which he could pass as a clerk or canvasser, or, by changing his demeanour, as a mechanic in the crowd outside a Labour Exchange. Spiv and Wally got up with him. "You got all the points?" Barney asked him. "Down the side-passage, to the back entrance. But not the back door or the back window. The side window— a sort of cellar or larder. That one's as easy as treacle. He collects the stuff in a little black case, and he takes it upstairs with him. I got that from the maid. It'll be all clear for yuh, 'cos Monday's her afternoon out."

"That's all right, Barney. I've as good as got it. Come on, now—let's go."

They slipped out of the house with the easy air of three young men taking a stroll, leaving Barney and Flaming Florrie glowering at each other. With the idea of lightening the thunderous atmosphere, Barney set about entertaining her with the story of his life, until she threatened to set about *him*; when he went to sleep. The three young men went to Ilford.

When they reached Ilford, they separated. Spiv and Barney went for a walk down the neat little road where the selected house stood, and Young Fred went straight to the house with an air of open business. Following Barney's advice, he went to the side-passage, closed the little garden door behind him, and stood for a minute at the kitchen-door as one waiting for admission. Then he went to the little window, and found its catch as Barney had said, as loose as treacle. Had there been any observers, none would have seen him get through the window. At one moment he was on the ground; the next moment he was in the house.

He had the plan of it in his head, and his rubber-soled shoes made movement easy. He moved from the little cellar into the hall, and stood listening. The house was as still as a church. The doors of two rooms—a little dining-room and a little parlour—stood ajar. He peeped into each, and found them unoccupied. They contained nothing that he could easily carry; nothing, indeed, that was of any value. He deduced that the old man, like many owners of small property, was a grubber, if not a miser; one who collected money as other people collect curios, and was not particular about home-comforts if home-comforts meant expense.

He slid up the stairs as lightly and swiftly as a boy slides down the banisters. He stood on the landing and listened. His muscles and sinews were lithe and ready for any movement, but none was asked of him. The house was still, and the only live presence that reached him was its musty smell, which seemed to be its soul. He could feel that smell through other senses than the nose. The landing showed two closed doors, but he gave them only a glance. Barney had mentioned the front room as the old man's bedroom, and the door of the front room was half open. He slid to it, and put an eye round the door. The room was empty, but there, at the side of the bed, was the black case. He chuckled. This was jammy; very jammy. Flaming Florrie would have to change her tone this evening, though he wouldn't tell her how really jammy the thing had been.

He put one foot inside the doorway, and with gloved hands reached for the case. With a deft movement he opened it, and saw packets of nice pound-notes and nice ten-shilling notes, and two still nicer fivers. In twenty seconds the packets were in his pockets, and the case was shut and back in its position by the bed. He slid along the passage to the stairs, and was just swinging round the stair-rail to go down when a hoarse voice, almost at his elbow, said "Here—you—hi!—come here——"

Over his shoulder he saw that one of the closed doors had opened. He had a glimpse of a hairy torso, half-wrapped in a bath-towel; then a hairy arm shot out of the towel to his collar. He dodged it, and gave a push at the bath-towel which sent it and its contents to the floor. He shot down the stairs, and out by the front door. He went with an easy stroll down the yard or two of front garden, and easily, but a little more briskly, went towards the main road. Four or five people were about, but none of them noticed Young Fred. Even when a clamour arose, they paid more attention to the maker of the clamour than to him. When an elderly male figure, naked save for a bath-towel, shot out of one of the houses and ran towards Young Fred, shouting "Hi—hi!" and when Young Fred began to run, the passers-by urged him to run under the impression that an elderly lunatic was menacing his male nurse. Three of them began to chase, not Young Fred, but the bath-towel; and even when the bath-towel raised the cry of "Stop thief!" there were only two citizens in that road who were public-spirited enough to pay attention to it.

These two were Wally and Spiv. As Fred came flying down the road, the lanky Wally tackled him first. He made a diving dash at the thief, and caught him round the waist. But the thief easily flung him off on his back, and when Wally scrambled up and made a show of rubbing his shin and dusting himself, his inner pocket was stuffed with packets of notes. Towards the end of the road Spiv heard the cry, and turned. As the flying Fred came at him, Spiv ran alongside, and made a weak grapple. Spiv was a little chap, and the onlookers admired his pluck; but it was fruitless. After a wrestle this way and that, he was tripped and flung on his face; and when he was able to get up the rest of the notes were under his belt.

Police-whistles began to be heard. Doors opened, and housewives and old men came out. Wally and Spiv, two strangers united by their public spirit, exchanged notes, and told the onlookers what they had tried to do, and then limped together to the main road to see if the wretch was caught. Spiv muttered advice. "Not too quick, Wally—not too quick. Be just interested, like." When they reached the main road he let out a low whistle. "Cor—look at the crowd. What d'you bet they ain't got him?"

Wally, who was taller, re-assured him. "No. That ain't for him. It's only a Punch-and-Judy show."

"But they're all looking this way."

"Ah, but that's on'y the police-whistles. Thank God there *is* a crowd, anyway. We can melt in. Let's join it."

"But where's he got to? Can't see no sign of him. Can you?"

"No. There's a busy jumping on a bus there. But he wouldn't be such a fool as to get a bus."

"Not him."

"And there's one stopping a private car. Think he's pinched somebody's car?"

"Not likely. Not when he's chased. That's a mug's trick when you're chased. He knows better ones than that. But let's duck in the crowd. Duck in, and change hats."

So they ducked into the crowd of school-children and mothers and old men, round the Punch-and-Judy show; and their soft hats went into their pockets, and by the process of putting on tweed caps they became different young men with different faces. The busies were busy in a way that would have gratified Isaac Watts and Samuel Smiles, sixty-seven householders having obeyed official instructions for emergencies, and Dialled 999. But Spiv and Wally were safe. The chase went past their little crowd, eastward out of London and left the road to Stratford and Mile End clear.

They paid little attention to the show, but they noted that the performer was working hard. Possibly he knew that police-whistles are a greater magnet to a crowd than any everyday entertainment, and so tried to hold his little audience by extra gusto. Spiv and Wally pretended a keen interest in the show, and kept their faces turned towards it; but their eyes went swivelling to right and left and rear, watching the doings of the busies and skinning the townscape for a sight of Young Fred. The show went through its usual incoherent course, but with somewhat more noise. Punch squeaked and squawked, and Judy groaned and grunted and gasped, and the little white Toby barked like a highly-trained house-dog at sight of a tramp.

"No good waiting here," Wally said. "Better be getting back, hadn't we? We can't do nothing here."

Spiv, with more knowledge of the great outdoors of London, said, "No. Don't move yet. There's still a couple o' blueskins buzzing about. And that shabby bloke over there in the mackintosh—I seen him before. He's one o' the mobile gang."

So they stayed and watched the centuries-old drama played out almost to its end. Punch was walloped by Judy, and in turn he walloped her, and bashed the policeman, and insulted the judge with all manner of loud and low noises. But when Punch should have hanged the hangman, either the performer was tired or he knew his public. Anyway, he held the climax in suspense and made an interval for a collection. Over the sill of the box came a collecting-bag on a long pole. It moved here and there among the crowd, its gaping mouth pathetically soliciting pennies. It was fed with one or two, but the bulk of the crowd followed its example and moved here and there upon their respective affairs.

Spiv and Wally took the opportunity of joining a quar-
tette of mothers and children, and walked level with
them in the part of respectable young fathers.

At the Broadway, where the crowd was thicker, they
dropped their parts and met at the bus stop. "Your
stuff all right?" Wally asked. Spiv said it was, and asked
how much Wally had. Wally said he didn't know. By
the feel of it, there must be about thirty pound-notes.
Spiv said his felt more than that. "We must a-got
between us about seventy or eighty. I hope," he added,
"that nothing's happened to him." He said it in so
sincere a tone that Wally gave him a close look.

"And if something *has* happened to him?"

"Why, then we should—I mean, I suppose we'd just
hand it over to Florrie."

Wally considered this. "Yes, I suppose we should.
But then"—with an airy shake of the head and a melancholy tone—"nothing *has* happened to him. He'll be
there when we get back. Things don't happen like that.
Still, it's a bit queer. He always was a quick melter,
but I never see anything like that. Just faded out like
cigarette smoke."

"Ah. Thirty pounds on you. And forty pounds on
me. P'raps more."

The lanky Wally sighed. "Yes. We shan't know how
much until it's counted. And we can't count it till we
get home. And then—Flaming Florrie will count it
for us."

"Yuh." Spiv accepted the inevitable, and on the ride
back to Mile End, and from there, through side-streets,
to Commercial Road, he and Wally devised dreams upon
the fantastic themes of thirty pounds and forty pounds—
dreams in which the long white arm and the fierce hand
of Flaming Florrie played the part of rude alarum.

When they did get home, and dutifully turned out
their pockets, she was as fierce as if they hadn't. She
had had four hours of Barney, asleep and awake, and
all that she had been saving up for Young Fred was let

H

out on Spiv and Wally. "That's the stuff, is it? All of it? Honest to God? Eighty-three pounds. Not bad. But where's Fred? What yuh done with him?"

Spiv, who had no real fear of Florrie's hand, since her hand, whether as bruise or blessing, was to him equally worshipful, answered for himself and Wally. "He slipped us. We lost him."

"Lost him?" Flaming Florrie flamed. "What yuh mean—lost him?"

"Well, we—we—lost him. He just skinned. He's prob'ly somewhere behind."

"Is he? So'll I be with you if you've let him get pinched. What yuh done with him? What happened on the job?"

"Well, he just skinned."

"What I'd like to do to you, if you wasn't already a couple o' rabbit-skins. What did yuh do to cover him?"

"We couldn't do nothing. He came out o' the house, passed us the bunce, and just went out like a bit o' smoke. We never saw him again."

. Florrie glowered, and shook her head and her mane at them. "I always knew Fred was a fool. Taking a dose of mumps like you with him. I'd rather have the face-ache any day than you two and Barney. You were supposed to help him, weren't yuh?"

"But how could we? He just went out like nothing, and we thought he'd got right away and'd be here when we got back. I see him one second, after he'd put me down with the stuff. And when I looked round, he warn't there."

"Warn't he? And I wish you warn't *here*. Get out and look for him. Go and arst about him. See if any of the other boys a-seen him. Think what happened to Crack Milligan."

"Ah, yes, Florrie, but Crack Milligan had some stuff. Fred ain't got any stuff on him. *We* got it. And nobody'd out Fred just for himself alone—now would they?"

"How d'you know? You got no place to be rude to Fred. There's more people'd think of murdering Fred than'd ever think of murdering a couple o' squirts like you and Wally. Even if you *had* got one-and-tuppence on yuh. If I wanted to murder anyone, I'd sooner murder Fred than——"

She stopped on the bang of the front door, and the entrance of Young Fred. He came in with an elated step. He tossed an evening paper to the table, and looked over the stuff deposited by Spiv and Wally. He strutted, and was bold enough to jerk his head at Florrie, and grin. She gave a look of relief at his entrance, and then, to cover her shame, she barked at him. "What you been mucking about at, you dough-nut? Back at six, you said. And look at the time. Where yuh been?"

"I been busy. Couldn't get away before." He nodded to Spiv and Wally. "You boys did good work. We'll make a fair split o' this."

"But Fred, where'd yuh get to? How'd yuh skin out, the way yuh did?"

Young Fred did another strut, and pointed to the front page of the evening paper. They gathered round it and saw an Ilford story:

. . . one of the oldest men in the business. He stated that he had just begun his show when he received from somewhere a blow on the head which stunned him. He knew nothing more until the police revived him when they came to order him to move his show away, which had been standing for two hours. It is thought, however, that his collapse must have affected his memory, and that he received the blow much later, since two or three people say that he went through his performance almost to the end.

"Well?" Young Fred squeaked with excited pride. "What yuh got to say now, Florrie? Have I mucked it?"

Florrie frowned at him. "Y'know, Fred, I'm sometimes bothered about you. There's times when I almost begin to think you got brains." ·

Fred grinned. "And you ain't far wrong. And I got a first-class squeak, ain't I, boys? I put it over you and everybody—'cept the dog."

BEAUTIFUL DOLL

THROUGH London streets which were darker even than the London streets of Chaucer's time, Hugo Floom, the white-haired professor of philosophy, was pursuing, in the early months of the war, his favourite pastime of night-wandering. He rather liked walking in the black-out. In those early months it was a novelty and he found it friendly to reverie and to disconnected thought, since it shut out so many of the world's distractions. And it was kind to one's sensibilities, since one couldn't see so many ugly faces.

As he fumbled his way through one of the shopping streets of the West End, he made a soft collision with two smartly-dressed men who were coming from the side entrance of a small but expensive grocery-store. They came out casually, but with alert movements; after a pause, they went at a steady pace towards Oxford Street. In the moment of their passing, he heard one of them say: "Think it'll be all right?" and heard the other reply: "Sure. Much better than our pockets. In case we were frisked. We can send Arthur in on Saturday to buy it, and get them to deliver it. Then it'll be their own affair."

He gave the men only a perfunctory glance, and walked on. He had noticed that people walking in the black-out, since they could not be seen, were more talkative than in the lighted streets of peace. He had several times amused himself by piecing together the disjointed scraps of conversation that fell from one shadowy passer-by and another, and trying to make a story of them. Usually he failed in making even sense of them. That very evening, in his slow walk from the Strand, he had picked up two good specimens, and he tried to link them with the remark he had just heard. One had come from a man in white tie and tails: "Yes, Elaine always has ideas. She gave Philip a street-organ for his birthday, and. . . ." The other came from a dim figure in Upper Brook Street: "Well, of course, he couldn't keep a zebra in his bedroom, so he had to . . ."

As he walked home to Regent's Park, he tried to create a story about a family circle in which Arthur bought the groceries, Philip went round the streets with an organ, and the youngest brother kept zebras. It came to nothing, and he thought no more of any of the remarks until the next evening.

He had an appointment that evening—seven o'clock Piccadilly Circus, outside the Tube station—with a friend. Seven o'clock came, and seven-fifteen, and seven-thirty, but no friend. He didn't bother to go and look for him at other entrances to the station. He had learned that looking for a missing friend in the black-out is as maddening as looking in a Welsh telephone directory for the number of a man named Jones, when you have forgotten his front name and only know his street address. So he stood still, and invoked patience, and listened to the scraps of talk which the darkness threw to him. One scrap came from two young men: "I told you how it'd be. I looked in the window and the damn thing's gone. All through you. I always say Do It Now, and you're always so fond of procreation. . . ."

"You mean I take things easy, and put 'em off. Educated people call it procrastination."

"I don't care what they call it. It's much too good a name for *you*, you bl . . ."

At that moment Floom saw his friend approaching. He had known him only a few months. He had met him at the entrance to a bar, where they had got into a tangle in playing that game of puss-in-the-corner which one has to play when two people are trying to find a way in and a way out round the three or four mazy fences that screen our bar doorways to-day. He had taken a liking to young Mistral—to his ardour, his unbridled good-nature, his mad doings, and his bawdy stories. Though

Mistral lived in Chelsea, and was the son of an artist—at least of an R.A.—he was really quite a good painter. By his landscapes he earned as much as a hundred pounds a year, but his wife had such expensive tastes that he greedily increased this income by doing drawings for an advertising agency, from whom he got no less than four guineas a drawing, less commission to the agency.

As he approached the Tube entrance, Floom noted that he had with him a lady, and a quick flash of his torch showed him that this lady was not the artist's wife. Further, the artist was singing, which Floom had never known him do in his wife's presence. The wife had ideas of music and *bel canto*, and favoured no composer later than Palestrina, and approved no singing later than that of people she could never have heard. She would certainly not have approved the artist's vocal efforts, since he was singing one of the latest Spanish popular songs, which, like the latest English popular songs, and any other popular songs, had come from America.

The lady whose arm he held appeared to be faint. Floom did not like to think of an alternative explanation, though he was familiar with the ways of young ladies in literary and art circles. So, as the artist was supporting the young lady, almost lifting her along the pavement, he assumed that she had perhaps twisted her ankle in the black-out, or had an attack of night-blindness. But while he knew that young Mistral had different ways of doing most things, he was at a loss to guess why the artist should suppose that an American song, delivered in an unseemly falsetto, would help to bring the lady round.

But by that time they had met. Mistral threw an arm in the air which was just loose enough to escape being an unpopular form of salute, and yelled: "Hullo, old boy!" Since his friend was accompanied by a lady, though a faint lady, Floom raised his hat, and said "Good evening," and at once saw that it was Mistral who was in the alternative state. "Hullo, old boy—I've just bought this! How d'ye like her?"

Floom, in spite of many years spent among philosophers, was privately as respectable as a Permanent Under-Secretary, and he met the remark with a little cough. "Ah—'m—you've just *bought*. . . . Really!" Then he remembered that Mistral had a habit, common among painters, of ignoring what we call delicacy and they themselves call humbug. He had a habit of telling the Anglo-Saxon truth.

"Yes. Just bought her. Don't you think Joan will adore her?"

Floom hesitated. In his experience of life, including the curious life he encountered in his own vivid imagination, he could recall no instance of a wife adoring her husband's casual mistress. "Well," he said, wrapping himself up in one of those meaningless phrases that are such a help in awkward moments: "Well, it all depends."

Mistral agreed. "It does. That's just the trouble. It depends. It's been depending on my arm for the last half-hour till I'm nearly sick of it. And I can't find a taxi anywhere. Grr-up, ye silly, pink-faced leprechaun!" And with that the artist landed a right hook into the fainting lady's stomach.

Floom stepped forward to protest with "Really, I say——" and then broke off. The lady, he saw, was no lady; she wasn't even somebody's wife; only a life-size doll dressed in the modern fashion. For a second or two he stared at it, and then at Mistral, with pursed lips. "But—but—really, my dear lad, what on earth are you doing, hawking a thing like that round the streets, when we're supposed to be going to dinner? Has Joan got tired of posing for your bathing advertisements, that you have to buy a lay figure?"

Mistral gave it another punch. "Good, isn't she? I've christened her Dulcinea. She isn't a lay figure. She's bung full of chocolates. And only four-pound-ten."

"Really! But four-pound-ten seems rather a lot for a box of chocolates in these times. Have you been at—what do they call it?—playing the dogs? Or, since all values are exploded, have you sold a picture?"

"No. But it's Joan's birthday. And it isn't really dear. It's so—so—l-life-like. Look at the expression. And the pose of the head. Just the way Joan holds her head when she's going to spill the dirt on me. There's real art in that modelling. And you have to pay for art. Though of course art doesn't really Pay. Or I wouldn't be living at Chelsea, and going without Burgundy. I don't mind going without things, as long as they're things I don't want, but when it comes to Burgundy. . . . Anyway, I saw Dulcinea in the window, and I couldn't resist her. She's so good that at the last pub where I tried to get a drink, they wouldn't serve me. Said my lady friend wasn't in a state to be seen on licensed premises. But I'm getting sick of carrying her. I can't get a taxi, and they won't let me take her on a bus."

"But why carry it? Why didn't you have it sent?"

"Because they wouldn't have sent her till to-morrow morning. And Joan's birthday's to-day. And I'd forgotten all about it till I saw Dulcinea in the window. Then the pose of the head reminded me. And as I'd just got the amount—I'd just drawn the payment for this week's drawing, and I had a few shillings left—I dashed in and got it."

"I see. Well, I hope Joan'll think it was worth four-pound-ten. Though I wonder how you're going to live next week. Anyway, where are we going to dine—with a thing like that with us?"

"Well, I thought we'd go to Chelsea, and park it at the flat, and then have dinner in King's Road somewhere."

"If you think I'm going to make myself so ridiculous as to walk through the streets with *that*—even in a black-out—just to dine in King's Road—you're mistaken. We'd better put off the dinner, and make it another night, without Dulcinea."

But at that moment it appeared that they would be relieved of the company of Dulcinea. Out of the black nowhere sprang two hefty young men. One of them gave a husky order—"Now! Get his legs!" His companion swooped and grabbed Mistral round the legs, while the first man made a snatch at Dulcinea. Mistral let out a yell, and went to his knees. But he held on to Dulcinea with one arm, and with the other gave one of the attackers a blow that made him bend and gasp. Then he writhed out of the grip of the other man, and staggered to his feet with "Here! What's all this? Hi—Floom—help!" Floom went between them and raised his stick. He wasn't so used to physical encounters as Chelsea artists are, and wasn't certain what to do. He could only say—"Look here—you, sir—unwarranted assault. I'm a witness, remember. Where's a policeman?"

The husky man barked at him. "Shut-up—we're having no police here. It's our mascot."

Mistral made a flying kick at his rear. "It's not. It's my wife's birthday."

"It belongs to us."

"It don't. I bought it."

The two men crowded Mistral again, and Floom again got between them, and having no police whistle, gave an ordinary whistle which he meant to be piercing, and which penetrated about six yards. The men tried to edge them into Haymarket, and Floom saw a car draw up, driven by a girl with a loose mouth and hard eyes. Mistral jammed Dulcinea against the wall, and planted himself in front of her, feinting with his left. "Now then—if you chaps are out on a rag, all right. Only you'd better look out. I've been in a few Chelsea Arts Balls. And Quat'z Arts Balls. And I've got to get this thing home. This is a domestic affair."

"I tell you it's our mascot. Better hand it over quiet. Make any trouble——" the husky man came closer, and Mistral poised himself for a blow; "—make any trouble, and we'll cut yuh into fifty pieces, and tear yer heart out, you——" He finished in a stream of odious words. "Now then—going to hand over?"

"No."

The man made a spring, and seeing that he was dealing not with raggers but with ruffians, Mistral shot out a foot. The man went down. The other came on, and the girl got out of the car, and was moving across the pavement to get along the wall and take Mistral at the side, when Dulcinea and he were saved.

Before either of them were near him, the whole London sky was rent with that blue and agonised howl which never could have tempted Ulysses to turn his ship. Two air-raid wardens dashed along, and called to them. "Turn off your headlights—you with the car. Get it away from here." The wardens waited to see them do it, and Mistral caught Floom by the sleeve. "Quick—into Jermyn Street. And then up the court into Piccadilly. We can dodge 'em there."

.   .   .   .   .

They had to walk all the way to Chelsea, which they reached with the All Clear. Floom would have liked to go home, but Mistral was insistent that, as a friend, he ought to keep him company as additional protection to Dulcinea. Floom didn't want any more ragging parties, and he particularly didn't want to go with Mistral in his present state. He knew from experience that whenever a sober man finds a friend in a hilarious condition, and takes him home, the wife at once assumes that it is *he* who has got her husband into that condition, and proceeds to hand him a few phrases straight off the ice. Mistral and his Joan did not at any time live very happily together; there was only, during the week, an occasional half-hour of wedded bliss. But in their case this was good for them. A happy love-affair is not of much use to an artist. It gives him no more inspiration than a boiled egg. Mistral's best work was done in an atmosphere of heartbreak and hell. But it didn't suit the elderly and placid Floom.

Still, there was no getting out of it. When, near Mistral's door, he hesitated, Mistral shouted "Come on, old chap!" and dragged both him and Dulcinea up the stairs.

The reception, as he had expected, was glacial. Joan was small, but she had hair of a thunderous black, and glittering eyes. She looked at her husband, and then at Dulcinea, and then at the friend. Her expression was that of a severe governess who had just bitten an unripe gooseberry. "What's this?"

"Dulcinea, my darling. And it's for you—with many, many hap-happy returns!"

"H'm. . . . Where did you get it?"

"Bought it. For *you*, darling—for you."

"H'm. . . . Where have you been all this time?"

"I been busy. Buying this and getting it home."

"Ha! And I've been waiting in all the afternoon for you. It's Friday, isn't it, and I wanted to do some shopping, and I've been waiting for some money."

"Money. . . . Ah, yes. . . . Take a look at Dulcinea, darling. Isn't she lovely?"

"Yes. Perfect. Wonderful. But I'd rather look at some money."

"Ah. . . . Yes. . . . Money. Of course. Well, I'm sorry, darling, but you see, being your birthday, and—and all that, I had to do something, and I'm afraid there won't be any money this week."

She put her feet together and folded her arms, and the action somehow turned him into an abashed schoolboy. "Oh . . . there won't, won't there? Indeed! And how much did you give for that idiotic thing?"

"Four-pound-ten, darling, and it's——"

"Four pou——"

"Yes, but you see, darling, it's bung full of chocolates. And they say they're going to be rationed."

"Is it indeed? And you, I can see, are bung full of something else." Here she sent a flash of sheet lightning at the innocent Floom; then went back to her husband. "Four pou— If you aren't the nastiest little toad anybody ever turned up—the horridest little brat that was ever reared. Why did they rear you? And why did I marry you? There must be insanity in our family. You pie-can! You slop of coffee-stall coffee! You plate of last week's porridge!"

"But, darling, don't go on like that. After all, it's your birthday. I had to get something for you, and nothing—n-nothing's too good for you. I had to do something about it."

"Only because you were tight. If you'd been sober you wouldn't have bought me anything—not even a bunch of violets. Here we are—with nothing in the house, and you blue our money on getting tight with your friends——" more sheet lightning for Floom; "——and then you blue next week's money on buying me a damn doll!"

"No—no, darling. Oh, no. I didn't spend anything on getting tight. And dear old Floom's nothing to do with it. I've only just met him. No. If I'm tight, old Stinker did that for me. Wouldn't let me spend a penny. Some brewery's just bought his Academy picture of Ruth Amid the Alien Corn. They thought it was barley. I thought it was asparagus. Anyway, darling, make it up and have a chocolate. You open it like this— see?—at the bosom. It looks like taking a liberty, per- haps, but Dulcinea's used to being mauled about. There's several pounds here and they're going to be rationed soon."

With the expert movements of the artist he began to undress Dulcinea. Then he pulled down the cardboard bosom, and there were indeed several pounds but not a single chocolate. Out of the bosom poured a shower of pound-notes, ten-shilling notes, half a dozen fivers, and a cascade of half-crowns and florins.

They stared at it with the dull eyes that people always give to the really unexpected. Mistral was the first to speak. "Wh-what's this?"

Joan snapped. "It looks like money to me."

"So it does." He picked up a handful. "And it is. Well!"

Joan snapped again. "Where did you say you bought it?"

"I didn't say. But I bought it at Wegg and Wiggleses."

"H'm. Haven't you seen the evening paper?"

"Why should I see the evening paper? And how? I've been listening for two hours to old Stinker's news—then I was buying Dulcinea for you—then I was fighting for her life—and then walking home through a barrage. I'm an evening paper myself."

"You flatter yourself. But if you'd seen the paper, you'd have seen that they had a burglary last night—Thursday. The safe was opened and all the day's money was taken."

Floom entered the talk with "A-ha!" Joan didn't give him lightning, but she glittered at him. "Well—what do you know?"

"Something I heard last night just outside their place. And something I heard just before Robin arrived. And then those two men that went for you . . . the same two men all the time. Instead of coming away with it, and perhaps having it found on them, they stuffed it in that. And then, I guess—from the bit I heard—they were going to send somebody to buy it, and have it sent home. Only Robin got there first."

Joan still glittered. "Two men . . . all the time . . . something you heard? Stuffed it? Explain!"

Floom explained. She shrugged. "Well, I don't see it helps *us* at all. There's still nothing in the house."

"No, darling," Mistral said. "But there's money."

"Not our money."

"Oh . . . well . . . they've got my four-pound-ten. And I didn't get any chocolates. Slip out and get some soaked mammon and some ganny—ganny—I mean some smoked salmon and some galantine, and——"

She folded her arms and turned away from him. "Mr. Floom—you appear to be sober." There was a slight stress on "appear". "What are we going to do about this?"

"Nothing to do that I can see except take it back to-morrow. You can't do anything to-night. Leave it till to-morrow."

Mistral took a rueful look at Dulcinea. "Four-pound-ten . . . and not even a chocolate. Surely there'd be no harm in a shilling or two for a bit of soaked mam——"

"No! You've had enough soaking to-day. Put it all back. And then go to bed."

He bent humbly to pick up the stuff and push it back into Dulcinea's bosom. Floom helped him.

A week later Floom met them in Pall Mall. Mistral was wearing a new suit so smartly cut that he seemed unable to live up to it. Joan had a new gown. Mistral hailed him with an air that was almost dignified. "Hullo, Hugo. You free for lunch? We're going to the Epicurean. Won't you join us?"

"Epicurean? Indeed? Things must be looking up in art. To be sure I'll join you. In spite of restrictions, the chefs of the Epicurean still enable one to eat. Did you manage to get that extraordinary doll back to Who's-it's?"

Mistral gave him an angelic smile, and then changed it to a pained frown. "I did. And they were almost rude. Before I could say anything they passed her back to me. Flatly refused to take her back. Said her face was scratched, her nose was cracked, and her neck broken. Said they never took back damaged articles. So of course I had to keep her."

THE BLACK STICK

RALLINPIPE was one of those men who pass most of their lives without experiencing any contact with the sensational. One could say that wherever Rallinpipe might be there would occur nothing but the smooth workings of well-ordered daily life. Fires happened in London, but in all his years he had never seen a house on fire. He had never seen a street-fight; never seen a man arrested; never seen a smash-and-grab raid. These things happened every day, but they could not happen in the atmosphere of tepid goodwill that Rallinpipe carried with him. Wherever he went, order and seemliness were the cue for all things and all people.

His life seemed to have been ordained in all its points by some silver fairy. Its course, through his fifty-eight years, had run so much on velvet, that one felt that the fairy had cried to the cruel world—Hands off! Do what you like, the fairy had ordered, to the other hundred-million nits, but don't you dare touch this one. He must never wait in the rain for a taxi. He must never have to ask for an overdraft. He must be protected always from cheap restaurants, middle-row seats in the theatre, bad tailors, grocer's sherry, rabbit bridge-players, mumps, bohemian clubs, and all the other ungainly horrors of this world.

The story of his years, in the large and in detail, gave ample proof that the attendant minions had fulfilled their charge. At least, until the summer of a few years ago, when, in the space of a few weeks, this composed life was brought into contact with not only violence but a series of human disasters.

A fixed item of his daily programme was a morning and afternoon walk around certain streets or in the Park. On these walks he invariably encountered, and for some distance accompanied, his friend Glinsand. Within that square mile which is all that some people know of London, they were familiar figures. To certain maunderers at club windows they were known as Sancho and the Don. Rallinpipe was short, dapper, round, and in all his movements compact. Glinsand was tall, loose, saturnine, and in all his movements agitated.

On a certain summer morning, Rallinpipe chose hat and gloves with care, and then, for he clung to the old habit of carrying a cane, examined the hall-stand. It held a variety of canes of all kinds—malacca canes, sword-canes, panama canes, gold-headed, silver-headed, jade-headed, amber-headed. Rallinpipe was a collector. Just now it was canes and sticks. But earlier he had had his enamels phase, his miniatures phase, his coins phase, his intaglios phase, and at one time had almost caused a breach of relations with his housekeeper by his ethnographical-carvings phase. Often his housekeeper had said that some of those things would one day have a nasty effect upon him. With those outlandish things you couldn't ever be sure. Some of the sticks in the stand gave her quite a "turn" by their very shape. She never touched them, even with a duster. She couldn't think what he wanted with such things. They might put horrible ideas into his head, and make him do wicked things without his knowing. Or might alter his character right through, like in a film she had seen about a doctor named Jekyll. He tried to reassure her, but she continued to treat the outlandish things with a distant and frigid air that gave them no encouragement to penetrate *her* psyche.

From the hall-stand this morning he chose a queer-looking black cane of Eastern design, a recent purchase that went well with his gloves and shoes. He then strolled out into the morning, down Brick Street, and into Piccadilly. Near Clarges Street, as usual, he encountered Glinsand, and they went across to the Green Park. They were getting well into an argument about the pilchard subsidy when they were stopped by a youth.

I

"Please, could you tell me where's the London Museum?"

Glinsand said, "No." He never knew where anything was, and was seldom sure where he was himself.

But Rallinpipe prided himself on his knowledge of this quarter of London, and his ignorance of all other quarters. "Yes, my lad." He swung his stick towards a corner of the Park. "Through the gate at that corner, and down a passage, and you'll come to it."

"Thank you."

The boy started off towards the gate, and they turned about and resumed their argument. They had gone but a few paces when Glinsand remarked that most of the other people in the Park were making towards that gate.

"Anything special on at the London Museum? Everybody seems to be hurrying as if—— Oh, look. Something's happened."

Rallinpipe turned and glanced towards the gate. A knot of people were gathered near it, and others were hastening to add tangles to the knot. "Come on, Rallinpipe, let's see——"

"Dear man, it's no affair of ours. Whatever it is— some vulgar accident, I suppose—it's the business of the park-keepers and the police. That's what they're for."

"No, but so few things happen. Do let's——"

"This vulgar curiosity of yours . . ."

"All that concerns human creatures, my friend, concerns me. Come on, do."

Rallinpipe allowed himself to be led, and when they reached the crowd he followed the thrusting form of Glinsand and found himself in the centre. The figure of what is officially called "a well-dressed man," lay prone on the grass. Glinsand stooped and rose. "Heavens, Rallinpipe, it's Old True Blue. Looks like a goner, too."

"Really, Glinsand—your terms. But I see it is—yes, True Blue of the F.O. So it is. A seizure, I surmise. Dear, dear. Is there no doctor to be——?"

Two policemen thrust them and the rest of the crowd aside. Ambulance men appeared in the little alley from Cleveland Row, and the inert form of Mr. True Blue was carried out of sight.

That afternoon the papers carried a story of the tragic death of that staunch veteran of the old school—struck down by the hand of a silent and invisible assassin. Examination had disclosed a small puncture at the back of the left ear, and from this puncture had spread instantaneous collapse of all the faculties. It was held at once to be the work of some foreign malcontent. For who else could have wished to harm this silver-haired, fiery-faced stalwart, who had fought so stoutly, and with such command of opprobrious terms, to keep the burden of power and wealth off the shoulders of the people of these islands, and on the shoulders of the few inured to the burden? One paper only took a different view. This objectionable and un-English sheet hinted that it would probably turn out to be *felo de se*, and that deceased had been stung to death by ingrowing class-epithets—a comment considered to be in such bad taste that in the West End the paper was sold out within an hour.

On the report of the tragedy to headquarters, every activity was begun to track and trap the assassin. All the known disaffected were held, and asked to give an account of themselves. All sea and air ports were watched. All dubious quarters were combed. Throughout the next day reports came in to Fleet Street from twenty suburbs of the sudden appearance of mysterious and un-English characters. Quiet, orderly burglars, prowling about for a daylight examination of front and back windows, were subjected to a lot of unearned persecution. Private detectives, pursuing their business of shadowing husbands suspected of infidelity, were pointed out to the police as worth watching. In one suburb the police were summoned by an old lady to arrest a surveyor who had just set up his theodolite; and in all suburbs unobtrusive loiterers, such as bookmakers' runners and peddlers of drugs, came in for a harrying time.

But all these activities were futile. The assassin remained silent and invisible, and the case of Old True Blue would have dropped from the news in a few days if the assassin had remained still as well. But he didn't. Old True Blue was put back on the front pages by the sudden, and similar, death of a Hyde Park orator whose speeches were equally virulent but were dyed, not in the buff and blue, but in the scarlet.

Rallinpipe and friend Glinsand were walking across the Park that Sunday afternoon to take tea with a mutual acquaintance at Queen's Gate. Rallinpipe had always passed rather hurriedly that concourse of orators which brightens the London Sunday. He considered the whole thing a deplorable manifestation of an equally deplorable democracy—not only coarse, but vulgar. But this afternoon a notably loud voice reached his ear and caused him to slacken. He turned to Glinsand.

"Well, well, well, we are indeed a tolerant people. Do you hear the dreadful things that man is saying about poor Old True Blue?"

"Which man?"

"That one," said Rallinpipe, waving his stick towards a large, bushy man with a flaming red neck-cloth.

"Good luck to him," Glinsand said. "It's gratifying to know that the English can sometimes be expressive. I don't mind what form the expression takes, so long as our national woodenness can sometimes—— Hullo, chap's ill. Look, he's——"

"Ah, let us go on. Overcome, I suppose, by his own fury. High blood pressure, no doubt. A just retribution. The lack of control among these——"

But Glinsand had thrust his way into the crowd, and was the first to catch the orator as he slumped from his little rostrum. The crowd pressed inward, and for a minute Rallinpipe lost sight of his friend. Then, a little dishevelled, Glinsand struggled out and rejoined him.

"He's done all right. Looks something like the other affair. Before the police got to him I just had time to notice a little puncture in the wrist. Well, we shall know to-morrow."

Monday's papers made a big splash of the story, but had to hedge a little in their denunciation of the silent and invisible assassin. In the case of Old True Blue, their line had been clear—anarchy and class war. This second case threw out that theory. The assassin seemed to be a wandering homicide with no serious purpose. That it was the work of the man who had slain Old True Blue appeared certain. The points in each case agreed. Death had come silently and unseen in a public place, and had left the same sign of its coming —a tiny puncture. They ran the story, linked with the earlier affair, for all that they could wring out of it. But there was very little to wring, and by Thursday it was almost a "cold" story. Then, on the afternoon of that day, the assassin kindly warmed it up for them by making not one more stroke, but two.

That afternoon, Rallinpipe and Glinsand happened to be walking up Dover Street. Noticing a figure on the other side of the street, Rallinpipe pointed him out to Glinsand as the *maître d'hôtel* of a newly-opened restaurant who had agreed with Rallinpipe that the talk about oysters and summer was mere superstition. Ten seconds later, people in Dover Street began to move hastily, and, looking back, they saw the *maître d'hôtel* lying full length, half in the gutter and half on the pavement. Glinsand wanted to investigate, but this time Rallinpipe was firm and pulled him on. But personal investigation was unnecessary. Voices reached them from errand-boys and newsboys.

"Caw! It's another one. Little 'ole in 'is face."

Rallinpipe said, "Goodness—what next?" and shook it off his shoulders and walked on. Walked on into another tragedy. By various ways they got somehow into Grosvenor Square, and, to turn his mind from the sudden end of the restaurateur, Rallinpipe began deploring the present trend of things, as ten thousand other men of his age in that district were doing. "Dreadful, I think, the disappearance of the family house. Blocks of flats in Grosvenor Square. Look at that block they're rebuilding on the corner there." He waved his stick towards the block, and Glinsand nodded.

"Seems a pity, certainly," he said. "But London can't grow outward any more without losing touch with the centre. So it must grow upward. And anyway, these new blocks have a certain modern austerity that—I say, look—there's more trouble. That postman——"

A postman, passing the new block with a heavy sack, had just staggered, slumped, and fallen. His sack lay upon his head. This time Glinsand refused to be held back. "We must do something. Call police or something. There's nobody about—only that taxi—and that young feller. Hey—taxi!" But before they could reach the postman, the taxi-man and the young feller had reached him, and had examined him. The young feller was abrupt.

"Another one. Look at that puncture under the eye. You see anything of this happening? Any attack? I'm the *Evening Watchman*."

Glinsand said, "Are you? You were keeping a sharp look-out. You must have been nearer to him than anybody. How do we know you're the *Evening Watchman*?"

"Don't be silly. Come to that, you two were pretty much on the spot yourselves. This is pure chance for me—granted once in a lifetime to newspaper men. May I have your names?"

Rallinpipe snapped. "No you may not." He grabbed Glinsand's arm. "Come away, man, come away. Look—there's a whole string of people coming. Do let's go on."

He was right. The Square, empty a few seconds ago save for these four, was trickling with people. Disaster, with its own uncanny power of communication, was

pulling them in. Those who had seen nothing and heard
nothing seemed to know that something was happening in
Grosvenor Square, and they left their affairs and came
blindly to it. As they gathered, and a helmet was seen
bobbing among them, Glinsand allowed Rallinpipe to
lead him away.

"Quite upsetting," Rallinpipe said. "Dear, dear. In
the midst of life. . . . And in the midst of London. It
seems incredible. And two in the space of half an hour.
Here's myself, after a lifetime in which I've seen nothing
violent or dramatic, witnessing four tragic events in a
few days—all, as it were, under my nose. It's really
startling. Who can this creature be? Why, that deadly
missile might have taken one of us."

"Quite," said Glinsand. "A similar one might take
us even now. He can't be very far away. He might
indeed have meant that one for us. He might have
followed us from Dover Street."

"You don't think so? Really, in that case I think the
safest place is the club or one's home. Though there's
no escaping one's fate."

"True. But it's only sensible not to invite disaster.
So let's get a taxi."

They found a taxi in Mount Street, and Rallinpipe
dropped Glinsand at his Piccadilly club, and went on
to his own in Pall Mall, where he reduced four men to
glassy-eyed immobility and internal screaming by his
finely-detailed account of what he had seen and how it
had affected him.

For the next four days the newspapers, morning and
evening, ran a regular "Mysterious Assassin" story, and
set themselves to work up a first-class panic by repeated
and high-pitched assurance that there was no occasion
for panic. Sudden and secret death, stalking the streets
of London, was a dreadful thing. . . . The invisible
assassin, lurking at street corners, might daunt the
stoutest . . . and so on. . . . But the British public could
be trusted to remain calm, no matter how it was menaced,

and meantime the authorities were at work, and an early arrest could be looked for. This was no easy matter to handle (they said) and the fact that four cases had occurred so near to each other suggested the need for every precaution. But because there had been four cases, it did not necessarily follow that there would be more. Let us keep our heads, and, above all, no panic . . . no *panic* . . . no PANIC. . . .

There was, of course, no panic. There never is. The flesh-creepers of Fleet Street did their best, but their naïve efforts at scaring the public, and their naïve admiration when the public wouldn't be scared, are too regular a feature of journalism to merit remark. Even when the afternoon papers of the following Monday carried a story of yet another silent murder in the West End, the public did nothing but gather at the spot, as if each man hoped that it would be his turn next.

On the mid-day of that Monday, Pall Mall was astir with the arrival of men for lunch. Some were walking to their clubs, some were alighting at their clubs from taxis or from their own cars. Mr. Rallinpipe was walking. The day and the scene held nothing unusual. It was such a scene as he had observed every day for many years. Many of the men he saw were men he knew; others were men whose faces were familiar; and the rest were such people as would be seen in Pall Mall at any time. As he reached the steps of his club he noticed an acquaintance walking on the other side. The acquaintance nodded, and Rallinpipe acknowledged him with a wave of his stick, and went on through the glass doors to his pre-lunch glass of dry Manzanilla. Having slowly savoured that, and listened to the gossip from groups round about, he went to the dining-room, and set himself to the business of lunch.

He had got as far as a grilled bone when a young member entered in some hurry and joined a table near him. His eyes held news.

"You men heard? . . . No? . . . Another of those

murders. . . . Right outside. Here, in Pall Mall. And this time it's old Gilboddle—you know—Chairman of the what-ye-call-it Combine. True. Just getting out of his car at the Machiavelli. And went over—plonk. Smith, who's a member here, was passing at the time and caught him. Same thing as the others—little puncture in the forehead. Smith had a narrow escape—might have got *him*. What? Oh, about half an hour ago. Thought you'd have heard. I didn't see it—got it from the hall porter. You must have come in just before. Gets more and more queer, don't it? How the devil they're ever going to catch the fellow——"

Late that night, when Rallinpipe was sipping his usual midnight glass of hot milk, he had an unexpected visit from Glinsand. He was excited, and his arms and legs were even more like those of a marionette.

"Had to come round," he explained. "I've got things to say. Big things. These murders, y'know . . . Well, I've solved 'em."

Rallinpipe stared. "*You've* solved 'em," he said. "No."

Glinsand waved an arm. "I have. Completely. I gave all the afternoon and evening to it, and now I'm certain I've got it."

"What—*you?*" said Rallinpipe, unaware of revealing an opinion of his friend's intelligence. "*You*—after the press and the police have failed?"

"Yes—me. Mind you, there's no blame on the police or the press. They had nothing to go upon. I had just one thing, and now I've seen all the rest. These deaths, Rallinpipe, are not the work of a fiend or a madman. No. There's no vindictive purpose behind 'em, and no aberration. They're the result of chance."

"This sounds all very crazy."

"It may. But I can now locate and name the murderer."

"Indeed? But you always were cocksure about things. And what kind of man is he, this murderer?"

Glinsand stooped to his friend. "Look in the glass and you'll see him. It's yourself!"

Rallinpipe stepped back. "What on earth have you been drinking, man?"

Glinsand pointed a finger. "*Thou art the man!*"

"What *is* the matter with you? Is it over-study? Or have you been reading too many thrillers and identified yourself with 'em? All these dramatics——"

Glinsand relaxed, and appeared to change the subject. He pointed through the door at the hall-stand. "Where did you get that stick?"

Rallinpipe tossed his head and *tch'd*. "What are we going to have next? Where did I get that stick? When I was a boy it was a custom among street arabs to ask men where they got their hats. Is this a new form of that vulgar persiflage? And if so, what is it doing on your lips? You must be *quite* tight."

"No, Rallinpipe, I'm not. I ask for information."

"Which stick d'you mean?"

"That black one."

"I bought it somewhere. Some sale or other, a month or so ago."

"Ha!"

He went to the hall-stand, drew it out, and brought it into the room. He swung it idly in his hand, and looked at the walls. Rallinpipe watched him with friendly amusement. "I said, Rallinpipe, that these affairs were the result of chance. They were. But they turned on your bad manners."

"Bad manners! *Me?* Glinsand—to-morrow morning you will, I suppose, be sober, and prepared to apologise."

"Never. I mean I never will apologise. I'm sober now. But I shall not apologise, because the charge is true. I admit that it is the only touch of bad manners I have ever observed in you. But there it is—and it is a little fault that has had grave and grievous effects. I refer to your bad form in waving your stick towards things and people. You see that kakemono on the wall there."

"Which one?"

Glinsand swung the stick upwards. "That one."

In the enclosed stillness of the room they heard the faintest little noise of *pst*. Rallinpipe looked at his friend and said: "What was that?"

Glinsand said: "I knew it." He pushed him towards the kakemono. "It was *that*."

He pointed to a tiny puncture at one corner. He pushed the kakemono aside, and showed a similar puncture in the wall. He took out his pocket knife, and dug into the wall. He dug and scraped for some seconds. Then, on the blade of the knife, he offered a minute metal splinter. "There! There's the little carrier of sudden death."

Rallinpipe's lips opened, and his eyes stared. His pink brow went pale. "Good Lord above! And I——"

"Your stick, my friend, is a poison stick with an automatic release. Every time you swing it up at a certain angle the spring is freed, and it fires. See—like this. . . ."

Rallinpipe jumped to him. "Don't. Don't do it again. It makes me nervous. Oh-dear-oh-dear. I suppose you're right. I suppose that's how they happened. And to think that I of all people should. . . . How did you work it out? What made you think of me?"

"Why, I cast about for some factor common to each death besides the peculiar manner of it. And I found *three* other common factors."

"Really? Do you think anybody else—— But what were they?"

"One was that at each of those deaths you, who have never attracted violence, were present. Two—that on each occasion you were carrying that rather ugly stick. Three—that on each occasion you had the bad manners to use it for pointing at something."

Rallinpipe sat down and stared at an ash-tray. He stroked his head, and sighed. "Dear-dear-dear. The first time I've ever been accused of bad manners."

"Don't be too distressed about it, man. It's a little habit that may easily be overcome. I should break up that stick if I were you, and burn it. As for what your bad manners led to, the less said the better. Nobody can know but ourselves, and we'll forget it."

Rallinpipe rested his elbows on the table and stared at the wall. He muttered, "Dear-dear-dear. . . . Mmmmmm. . . . Dear-dear."

Glinsand patted him on the shoulder. "Come, man, don't let it get you down. I don't suppose anybody's noticed it. And you can easily master a bad habit—even at your age."

Rallinpipe appeared to be thinking of something else. "What?"

"I say you can easily cure yourself of that little bit of ill breeding. No need to brood on it."

Rallinpipe shook himself. "It wasn't that. As to breeding, I don't know that I'd take *you* as an arbiter, anyway. No; what I was thinking was the sheer waste. Those five harmless people. When almost any day in the Park there's that old onion the Bishop of You-know-where, and old Funspot of the *Pink Review*—and Muley-grubs of the Home Office—and . . ."

THE YELLOW BOX

YOUNG FRED was giving directions to his boys in his high-pitched voice. "It's a big yeller box. You can't mistake it. It's in the first-floor front room. A big yeller box—see?" He made wide gestures with his arms, and seemed to think he was demonstrating not only a size but a colour. "Yeller, see? A dirty yeller."

He was sitting with his boys in a back room of his home in the Regent's Canal quarter of London. Through the window came the night noises of the river— the suck of water against staples; the chugging of a patrol launch; the hoot of a late tug; the rattle of chains. In return, the window sent its gas-light to do a dreamy dance on the black water. "You got to get that box and bring it here."

His "boys" tried to look intelligent and looked like worried camels. "But how we going to get it?"

Young Fred looked at them with rat eyes and rat jaws. His affectionate name among his friends (who knew him better than his enemies) was Deadly Nightshade. At his look they drew back from the table. "Have I got to do all the work? Won't yuh never learn to walk without being held up? Use those bones yuh call yer brains. You, Spiv—and you, Barney—get that box and bring it here."

"What's in it?"

"What's that got to do wi' you? You'll see soon enough, and if yuh do the job prop'ly you'll have a share. Though I don't mind telling yuh now what's in it. Yuh can't do anything with it—a pack of slivers like you. Remember the job at Phillibrass Castle—gold plates, silver cups, and all? Crack Milligan's job? Well, that's what's in it."

They made admiring and reverent noises. "Gaw! . . . Coo! . . . 'Strewth! . . . But how did it get there?"

"Milligan planted it there. Wanted a safe place. He knows old Suey Lim, at that wooden house off the Causeway. I see the box there, and old Lim told me that Milligan had asked him to mind a box of clothes for him. I had a lift of it. Clothes! And I found he'd brought it in last Thursday—the very day after the job. Well, that's the box you got to get. It'll be quite easy. Nobody's looking after it. Old Lim thinks it's a box o' clothes. And he's out every evening from ten to past midnight for puck-a-poo."

"But, Fred! Milligan . . . if he finds it's gone . . . you know what he is. He'll guess it's somebody round here and he'll wipe up everybody."

Young Fred flashed his rat eyes at them and squeaked. "Will he? I shouldn't let him if I was you. Don't do to be too easy with people. It leads 'em on to take liberties. You got yer coshes, ain't yuh?"

"Yes, but Milligan——"

"Well, he's got a head, ain't he? And now shut up. It's half-past ten. At eleven o'clock you—Spiv and Barney—go and get that box, and bring it here. Wally can take a truck and keep look-out for yuh. Now clear out. I got to think where I can melt the stuff."

Half an hour later, Wally and Spiv and Barney were strolling separately past the decrepit and cringing cottages of the Causeway, through a tender mist charged with damp and dirt, fetid odours, and human hopes and fears. Wally was pushing a truck which held old iron, broken boots, and a few sacks. At the end of the Causeway they turned off into a street no wider than a passage. Spiv and Barney lingered near the top, and Wally went on pushing.

Fifteen minutes later, Spiv and Barney stood on the stairs of Suey Lim's little house in a cloud of ticking silence. They had a feeling that the darkness was stalking them and about to rush upon them. It was a foreigner's house and therefore, to them, capable of un-English surprises. It was clothed with an atmosphere of more than silence and darkness; a sense of something impending, which might or might not be human; might not even be alive. These foreigners . . . they had such tricks. They could charge all sorts of things with the power to harm. Both of them wished the job were done, and that they were back in the comfortable rat-faced society of Young Fred. This house held more than it told, and they felt this so keenly that when Barney put a soft hand on Spiv's shoulder, Spiv let out a strangled *Oush* and jumped down three steps.

Barney quieted him. "Shut up, yuh fool. The front room, he said, di'n he?"

"No, the back."

"The front, yuh fool."

"The back, I think."

"Shuttup. It was the front." They went up the remaining four stairs, and Barney, with a fat hand as light as a girl's, gently tried the door of the front room. It opened. He flashed a torch into the little room, and there against the wall, under the window, was the yellow box. "Come on, Spiv. Give's a hand, and let's get out o' here."

They crept into the room, and approached the big box. Spiv reached gingerly for a handle and gave it a lift. "Cor! What a weight! Must be fousands and fousands o' pounds worth o' stuff in there. We'll all be rich."

"Very likely. When Milligan does a job, he does it. Now then—oop!" With a strain of muscles they managed to raise it from the floor, and get their hands beneath it. Then, with staggering steps and gasping breath, they carried it on tip-toe to the top of the stairs. Spiv's knees were sagging. "Set it down half a mo. Whoo! Have to do it bit by bit."

"Urr. Heavier than I thought. Here—I'll get down three stairs, and you heave it on my back. I can manage it like that, if you hold up the tail end. Listen—what's that?"

They listened. A footstep cracked the silence of the street—a shuffling footstep, and with it a low whooping noise.

"All right—only Wheezy Jack going home. Now then—up with it."

Barney took it on his back, and they went with clumsy stealth down the stairs. Now that they had the box and were getting out, the darkness seemed to rush even more closely, and to be full of strangling fingers. But at last they were down. Barney slid the box from his shoulders. "Jump up, Spiv, and take a dekko through the fanlight. See where Wally is—if he's all clear."

Spiv climbed up on the box.

"Juss coming round the corner. All clear."

They opened the door. Wally brought up the truck, and together they hoisted the yellow box, and covered it with sacks and old boots. Barney went in front and pulled, and Spiv and Wally pushed. On the journey through the misty Causeway, where arrows of light shot from the crevices of the shuttered windows, and through the other byways, where the lamps were only faint yellow smears, they passed only two figures. The two figures passed them as though they were invisible.

Back at Young Fred's, they took no care about noise, and pulled and pushed the box into his lower room with much gasping but less strain. Young Fred showed no elation. He had no belief in enthusiasm, and he worked himself, and encouraged his boys to work, in a cold mood, never despairing and never doing the sillier thing of hoping. He looked at the box.

"Mmmm . . . One of his fancy locks. Well, other people knows about locks besides him." He went to a drawer, pulled it out, fished behind it, and brought out what might have been a surgeon's instrument-case. "See what you can do, Wally." He handed it over, "And don't be too long."

Wally opened the case, and took out three little instruments which would have been useless to a surgeon. He

went to work on the obvious lock, and tore its fittings
apart in ten seconds. Then he felt about the box for the
concealed locks; located them; and set to work on them.
The other three stood around him, seeing nothing in the
room save the box and his hands. For many minutes he
worked, eyes set and lips twisting. At last a little click
told that he had loosed the secret zone of one lock. After
that, the second lock had no secret. He sprang it and
lifted the heavy lid.

They moved forward in a bunch to feed their eyes with
the gold and silver treasures of Phillibrass Castle; and fed
their eyes with the doubled-up corpse of Crack Milligan.

They moved backward in a bunch with varied noises
of dismay, alarm, blasphemy, and disbelief. Then all
their feeling went into their faces, and they stared in
silence at the yellow box, with frowning eyes and
dropped lips.

Young Fred recovered first, and was just opening a
thin stream of corrosive words upon Barney and Spiv
when he remembered that it wasn't their fault. It was
the identical yellow box he had seen, and the yellow
box he had told them to get. It wasn't their fault, but
when things go wrong one must blame *somebody*, and
at the moment it seemed to him that only a couple of
idiots could be ordered to fetch a box of treasure, and
then fetch a box containing Crack Milligan, deceased.
Just as they were explaining that it wasn't their fault,
and he was admitting that it wasn't, there came one
solid rap of the front-door knocker. Young Fred slipped
to the shuttered window, pulled the shutter back one
inch, and put a hand-mirror at a slight angle into the
aperture. He turned to the others. "All right. On'y
Florrie. Let her in, Wally."

Flaming Florrie came in. Flaming Florrie's character
was in her name. She had a red head and a large
mouth. Her speech was as red as her head. Her short-
sleeved arm was as white and firm as alabaster, and her
hand as slender and fierce as a tiger's tongue. The boys

often said that they'd rather take a couple of upper-cuts from Young Fred's fist than a slap from Florrie's hand—all except Spiv, whose tastes were known to be peculiar.

Florrie looked them over and looked over them, which her stature enabled her to do. "Yuh got it, then? But what yuh standing round for like sick guinea-pigs? Isn't all the stuff there?" She went over to the box. Young Fred put out a hand.

"I shouldn't look at it if I was you."

"You would if you was me. And I'm going to."

She lifted the lid, and dropped it immediately. She pushed her mop of hair from her brow.

"Coo! No wonder you look like guinea-pigs. It almost give *me* a turn—not being ready for it, like. Why di'n yuh *say*?"

"You di'n give us a chance."

"Poor old Crack! Who done it?"

Young Fred waved his arms and squeaked. "How should I know? Not our job."

"No," said Barney. "We found it like that."

"Yes," Spiv said, being bright; "it come to pieces in our hands, like."

Florrie gave him a "Shut up, you," and turned to Young Fred. "What's it mean then?"

"It's Suey Lim's job—that's clear. The dirty double-crosser. Pretending to me he thought it was a box o' clothes!"

Florrie stared at the box. "Well, that was right enough. On'y he forgot to say there was something in the clothes."

"Grrr . . . But what we going to do now?"

"Dump it in the river," Spiv suggested.

Florrie cuffed him. "Baboon! That your best idea? Might as well dump it outside our door. Everything's found in the river. Besides, we ain't river people. Whose boat we going to get? Think o' something else, some of yuh."

They thought—or appeared to. Nothing came of the

process. Their minds and eyes were on the box and its contents, instead of the problem it presented. Then Florrie had an idea. "We got it by accident. Let someone else get it by accident."

"How?"

"Old George's gang. We can spread it that it's here—full of the stuff from the big job. And it is, too. And then you all go out one night, and let 'em see you out. I bet it'll be gone when you get back."

"But how yuh going to spread it? They won't take no notice if it's spread from us."

"Leave that to me. There's that angel-face in our street I've used once or twice. Little Elsie. Straight out of a Sunday-school prize. She can spread anything—as long as it's a secret."

Young Fred considered. "No. Too chancey." Spiv agreed with him. "Yes, too chancey"; which made Young Fred think of deciding that it wasn't. But he maintained his point. "No. George's lot might do something about it—even say where they got it, p'raps. Too chancey."

Florrie took three colossal strides of the room—all that it allowed—and three colossal strides back. She paused at the box. "Then there's only one thing to be done. Take it back where it came from—before he gets home."

Spiv and Barney broke out together. "Take it *back?* Back to that house——"

Florrie flamed at them. "Take it *back* was just what I said. D'yuh want me to——" They subsided. "That's the only thing. Get it back quick, and wipe yer finger-marks off it. And in future, Fred, stick to yer own job, and don't try to crash other people's. It never works—not reely. It's like playing tennis with a cricket-bat."

Spiv made another protest. "Well, let somebody else have a go. Me and Barney brought it. S'pose you and Fred do the return job and——" The rest of his sentence went with himself to the floor on the other side of the room, after a report like a stage pistol's. He got up, smoothing his face.

"You and Barney brought that box, and you and Barney'll take it back. And you'll *like* the journey. It's not raining. Now then!" She put her hands on her hips, and glowered. Spiv and Barney went to the box. Wally, without protest, went to get the truck.

Young Fred stood scratching his thin head. "What I'd like to know is what Suey Lim's done with the stuff."

Florrie swung an arm and barked. "You leave that stuff alone, Fred. There's a hoodoo on it. See what happened to old Crack, a chap that never made a mistake before. You leave it alone."

"P'raps you're right. But that Suey Lim—I won't forget this. Making such a fool of me. Working it acrost me. He must a-read my thoughts when he showed me that box."

"Wouldn't have taken him long, the way you play poker. You drop the whole thing, Fred. Get this back where it came from and forget it. And keep yer mouth shut. See?"

"Yes. But things ain't too good just now. And if we could lay our hands——"

"Drop it, I say. Else I'll lay *my* hands——"

Young Fred dropped it. But next day it was brought back to his mind. At that populous corner where West India Dock Road meets East India Dock Road, he ran into two young men whom he knew as associates of Crack Milligan. He tried to display a sudden and earnest interest in the architectural features of Nicholas Hawksmoor's church tower, but they interrupted his study. "Oy!" Unable to escape, he turned to them. Their manner wore no hostility and no friendship. It never did. As rivals, his group and Milligan's group had always shown each other that cool, imperial civility shown by one heavy-weight to another at the weighing-in ceremony. "Seen anything of old Crack lately?"

Young Fred hesitated. "Well, yes. No."

"What yuh mean—yes, no?"

"Well, not to speak to. I mean I seen him—at a distance, like."

"We ain't seen him for days. He ain't in any o' the usual places. And there's some business he was going to settle. He can't be in the cooler or we should have heard."

"No. He wouldn't be there."

"Well, where was it yeh seen him?"

"Oh, round 'ere somewhere. But I'll tell yeh where yeh *might* find him. Or hear of him."

"Where?"

"Know Suey Lim's place?"

"Heard of it."

"Well, he's been using it lately."

"Working with him?"

"Not as far as I know. But he's hanging about there. If you boys go round there, you might hear of him. If you go inside, you might find him."

"Righto. Thanks. We'll go along. We got to find him. It's—it's urgent."

They went off, and again Fred cleared his mind of the matter. But that same night it was again forced upon him. Spiv, who, among other accomplishments, was able to run while appearing to walk, came at electric speed through twisting alleys to Young Fred's home. "He's got rid of it."

"Who has—what?"

"Suey Lim. The yeller box."

"Blast the yeller box. How?"

"Done just what Florrie cuffed me for suggesting. Dumped it in the river. I see it come down from his window. You know the water comes right up to his back wall. He dumped it there. I see it sliding down on a rope. So there y'are, ye see. Them fellers, they got brains—cuter than ours, p'raps. Yet when *I* suggest the same idea, Florrie——"

"Oh, shut up. It's got nothing to do with us now. It's finished."

"No, but—the job we had getting it back. Up them stairs. When we could have——"

"Oh, leave it, yuh fool. It's all over. Florrie don't want it talked about. So don't say nothing to her. Let it drop. Let's go and have one, 'fore they close."

So they went to the Blue Lantern, and got there fifteen minutes before closing-time, and had more than one. They had more than one because Young Fred didn't take his own advice, and let it drop. The extra "ones" came from his letting himself talk on the forbidden topic. They were enjoying the first one with the usual expression of mourning that constant companions wear when drinking together, when Young Fred was tapped on the shoulder.

He turned and met the non-committal smile of a plain-clothes officer. He did not jerk away, or even blink. He fixed his rat eyes on the officer, and kept his mouth firm. The officer nodded. "Have a drink, Fred?"

"What's the racket now?"

"Oh, nothing. Just passing the time o' day—or night. Friendly-like."

"All right. Mine's a double whisky."

"Mmmm . . . One of those who can take any given quantity, eh? Well, I dare say it'll run to a double. And your pal?"

"He'll have a pint o' mild."

"Mmmm . . . letting me down easy on him. Well, here's a go. What's the news?"

"Ain't heard any. *I* don't go nosing about into other people's business."

"No? Then they must be slandering you about here. Well, you done that one pretty quick. Got room for another?"

Young Fred gave an emphatic "Yes," and then asked, "When's the shooting begin?"

The officer gave him a sardonic look. "Grouse shooting begins in August. Pheasants in October. Rabbits
we shoot any time."

"Well, shoot then."

The officer stretched his shoulders and looked at the
fly-specked ceiling. In the light tone of his other remarks
he said, "In re a yellow box."

Young Fred kept his hand steady and his eyes fixed.
In an equally light tone he said, "Well? What about a
yeller box?"

"Know anything about one?"

"No."

"Heard anything about one?"

Young Fred considered. Back to him came his disappointment and his wounded self-esteem over Suey
Lim's deception. He knew that for his own sake he
should have kept silent in the presence of authority, but
he couldn't. Looking intently at the counter, he said,
"Well, if you put it like that, I can't tell a lie." The
officer swallowed without intent, and coughed. "I don't
know what you want with a yeller box, or anything about
it, but I certainly have *heard* of a yeller box."

"And what might you have heard? If it's not betray-
ing a confidence?"

"I happen to have heard of a man that's *got* a yeller
box. Though of course there might be lots of yeller
boxes about."

"There might. But who might this chap be?"

"Old Suey Lim."

The officer looked disappointed. "Ah, . . . You mean
he *had* a yellow box."

"I mean he's *got* a yeller box."

"It's not there."

"What? Have you been—— Anyway, he *has* got it.
Not far off his place."

"Whereabouts?"

"I only know that my pal happened to mention that
he'd seen it."

"Ha! Well, if it's not far away, perhaps it's not too far for you and your pal to walk on a fine night like this?"

"Well, I dessay we could. If there's time for another before we start."

"We'll make time. . . . There you are. And a pint of mild for your pal. His face seems familiar. Reminds me of my old district—more fruity than this—Notting Dale. . . . Well, here's a go. It's good of you to tell us about Suey Lim. You're not usually so obliging with confidences."

"No, but Suey Lim was rude to me once. And while I can put up with a lot o' things, I can't put up with bad manners."

"Ah. That comes of living with Flaming Florrie, I suppose. They do say that women have a refining influence. But you always were sensitive, weren't you?"

"Always. It's a bit of a handicap"—he gave the officer a hard look—"considering the people one has to meet sometimes."

"I suppose it is. But you overcome it pretty well. No one'd ever guess. But let's go."

They went. Once or twice Spiv nudged Young Fred. "Here—what's this? I don't like this. What we doing this for? Suppose——" Fred told him to shut up and do as he was told.

They went through a tangle of half-lit streets and unlit courts; through shades of blackness from old bronze to ebony. They went across a roaring main road, and through wretched byways too bleak and querulous for pity. They went along a narrow lane by the waterside, cluttered with the day's refuse. On the way, the officer picked up two uniformed men who fell in behind them. Young Fred noted them, and wished he hadn't come. Spiv noted them, and would have run if there was a clear way to run. He muttered to Young Fred. "You been a fool. What we getting into?" Young Fred told him to shut up, and then touched the officer on the arm. "I say—look here—I don't know why you want this yeller box, but me and my pal got nothing to do with it. All I know is——"

"That's all right, Fred. You keep with us. Soon as we get it we're going to open it, and I'd like you to be there."

Young Fred stopped short. "No, but—listen. Let's have this straight. You asked about a yeller box, and I told you Suey Lim had one, and I said my pal knew where he'd put it. That's all I know. Absolootly all. I got nothing to do with old Suey Lim, and I don't know nothing about his doings. See?"

"That's all right. I only mean you ought to be there, because there's a nice reward for information about the Phillibrass Castle stuff. And as you were kind enough to help us, and——"

"The what stuff? I dunno what yer talking about. I ain't got nothing to do with no stuff. I'm just showing yuh where Suey Lim put a yeller box. That's all I know about it. And I don't want anything to do with it. You can't put nothing on me."

"I wouldn't think of it, Fred. Not just now. But you keep with us, and lead on."

So they went on, and at last they came to the little street where Suey Lim's house stood, near one of the wharves. And they went out on the wharf, and the officer took the shrinking Spiv under his command, and together they climbed down under the wharf, and splashed along until they came to the wall under Suey Lim's house.

The officer turned to Spiv. "Now then?"

"Juss about here," Spiv said, "was where I see it plonked."

The officer called to the men above. "Show us your lanterns." They sent the beams of their lanterns down to the water. The officer went a step or two into it. "I can see the end of a bit of rope here." He took off his coat, and rolled up his sleeve, and plunged his arm down. "Just slipped off when he sunk it, I suppose. We shall have to dredge in the mud for the box. Got it. . . . It's not

loose, though. It's caught on something. Here—you—
give us a hand. Pull with me."

Spiv and he pulled together. The rope was not caught
on anything firm. It gave to their pull, and began to
come to them slowly, inch by inch, and when ten feet had
come in, they saw, on its end, the box. The officer
grunted. "Lord—what a weight. Must be the whole
doings of the job in here."

Spiv shivered. "Ah, yes . . ." and was going to add
further words which were luckily stopped by a squeak
from Young Fred. "Here—don't take all night over it.
I don't want to be here when Suey Lim comes back. I
don't want to be served—— And remember, we got
nothing to do with this. We don't know nothing about no
Castle stuff, me and Spiv. And don't want to know nothing. I only told you about a yeller box because——"

The officer calmed him. "That's all right, Young Fred.
I'll see nobody hurts you. Very public-spirited of you to
turn in the reward. . . . We got it now. Turn it upsides.
Come down, Smith, with your lantern. . . . Mmm . . .
not much of a lock. Been tampered with. Soon have
that off."

He took a little tool from his pocket, and thrust it into
the lock. There was a sharp click, and the lock gave.
Under the light of the two lanterns, he lifted the lid.

He and his men expected to see one sight. Young Fred
and Spiv expected to see another. Both sides got a shock.
They saw neither the Phillibrass Castle stuff nor the body
of Crack Milligan. Young Fred saw that Milligan's pals
had carried out their search for him. Everybody saw
inside the yellow box the body of Suey Lim.

Lightning Source UK Ltd.
Milton Keynes UK
UKHW011448200921
390901UK00004B/1384